KINGSTOWN BURNING

RACHELLE J. GRAY

LadyGray
Publishing

Address correspondence to:

LadyGray Publishing

2340 NW 72nd Ave. B103

Fort Lauderdale, FL 33313

First Edition, September 2020

Printed in the United States of America

This is a work of fiction. Any resemblance to actual persons, living or dead, or actual events is purely coincidental.

Cover design by Box of Wolves

Edited by Make Your Mark Publishing Solutions

Interior design by hDigitals

Author photo by Indica Gray-Blackman

Map illustration by www.vectorgrove.com

"Wildfire" (Protect Me People) by Tarrus Riley © 2010

Album *Major & Minor Riddim* (Don Corleon presents)

Tarrus Riley lyrics are copyright by their rightful owner(s)

"One Draw" by Rita Marley © 1981

Shanachie – SH 5003

Rita Marley lyrics are copyright by their rightful owner(s)

ISBN 978-1-7350795-0-9 (Ebook)

ISBN 978-1-7350795-1-6 (Paperback)

ISBN 978-1-7350795-2-3 (Hardcover)

Library of Congress Control Number: 2020914658

Visit www.RachelleJGray.com

Instagram @ladygraysworld

Sans Dieu Rien.

I dedicate this book to Jah, through whom all blessings flow.
May He be pleased with my work.

This book is for Indica. My sun. Shine brilliantly.
To those who were so that I can be.
To everyone who listened, read, edited, believed, advised,
supported, guided, and encouraged me along this journey.
Thank you. Thank you. Thank you.

Blessed be Jah. Rastafari. Haile Selassie I.
His Majesty Livith!

CONTENTS

Caribbean

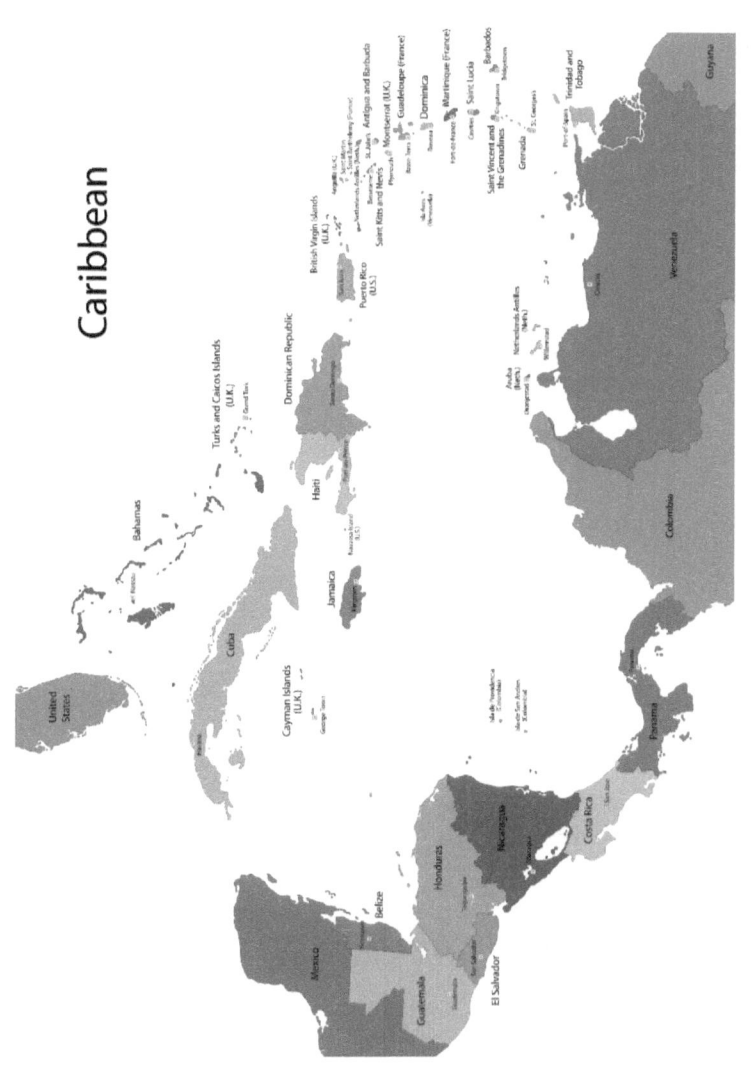

PART I

THE SHARK

Nubya was alone doing a graveyard shift in patience. Judah had left her to wait through his escape into the first sight of darkness.

Her thoughts fluttered about, agitated in their anxiousness. Unsettled, Nubya butted about the house, doing nothing and everything while her mind busied itself with endless scenarios on replay.

Driving herself mad in the twilight hours, she fought the temptation to check her cell for unread messages. Her ears yearned to hear familiar reassurances, while her tongue begged to be unleashed on her pity—if only just to stroke one of her mounds of insecurity.

It was a nasty brew, one that made Nubya feel less than a woman in those moments when she struggled to hold firm. Looking out of the kitchen window onto the backyard at the charred logs on the hearth, the scent of burnt mango wood softly wended its way across the yard, creeping in to mix with the remnants of the incense that perfumed her home. She tried to put on a pot and bravely cook a meal that would make her feel happy. But the heaviness of the evening crippled her. The bare knife lay there, impotent to dicing the provisions on the cutting board.

Above, a circling Regional Security Services patrol plane was making the countryside miserable. Blocks were on alert while smart devices gushed with coded dialogue and reported sightings. Weary village folk dozed uncomfortably in the sound of the plane's whining, resting in deep concern.

The raids were becoming more frequent, more intense, and less forgiving. In an attempt to look apt at stamping out "the bad seeds," Johnny Law moved through town and country, avoiding the heights and terraces in between, digging up lives, cutting down livelihoods, bent on finding examples to be made of.

"Hail de I!" a voice thundered out of the night.

"Rastafari live!"

"Hail, sis!" a greeting of love and respect floated in.

"Konjah Man." Relief tumbled out in Nubya's words as she identified the voice. The familiar sound lightened her heart. Nubya rushed to the side entrance of the backyard to buss the gate. Konjah Man stepped in purposefully, like he always carried himself.

"Tings hot tonight," was his response as his conversation slid by her silent questioning. "Judah not here?"

"Nah. He left with that Jamaican man I tell you 'bout. The one that is staying in the guesthouse down in Bamboo Valley."

Konjah Man appeared to think nothing of her words and continued on. She wanted him to think something of them but wasn't sure how to press the matter.

Everyone seemed mesmerized by this Jamaican man. A

tall, imposing character, he won over many with the high volume of charisma he exuded. He was a middle-aged man with an impressive crown of natties that told of his long years as a Rastafari. He wowed folks with detailed recounts of early persecution, gully trods, outlaw livity, and near-death experiences. How, in the mid-70s, as a young man waging guerrilla warfare against the system, Babylon had once caught and trimmed him.

His stories of dread, unlike the ones the elders from the surrounding areas told, always ended with the persecuted Rastaman rising above the oppression. The youngsters loved it. Ate up his tall tales underscored by a humble bravado as he imparted these little-known triumphs to clusters of curious youths chomping on his every word.

"Johnny Law making dem way 'cross here. I just hear that dem was over by Three Houses coming up. I tried to call Judah, but I ain't get him. So I pass through to sound the alarm," Konjah Man revealed.

Lost in her own thoughts, Nubya almost forgot that she was having a conversation. "They left here a while ago. I'm sure by now they must know 'bout that," she managed to respond, ending with a thought-filled pause that was pricked by the change of subject that followed.

"You got wrappers?" Konjah questioned as he frisked his body to bring forth chubby, short-blade scissors from his pants pocket and began cutting up a piece of bud cupped in his palm.

"Yeah."

"Hold this," he said, pinching off a smoke, then securing it with a half fold to the wrapper.

"Give thanks," Nubya responded with genuine appreciation.

"I knox a nice sap," Konjah suggested.

"Let me get two large ones," Nubya concurred.

Disappearing through the paling door, Konjah Man returned a while later with two steaming bio-bowls, which he handed over to Nubya at the door to her kitchen. Heading out into the backyard, he proceeded to perch on the edge of a bench, which sat under the sprawling mango tree that ruled the yard. From the kitchen window, Nubya could see the prelude to his desired outcome as he cast out seeds, rolled up the contents of the wrapper, and took his place amongst the fireflies.

The sap was too hot, and restlessness still tugged at Nubya. So she went into the yard and surveyed the sky. The night lacked personality; yet, so much seemed to be happening. She stoked the dying fire, then fidgeted with a few other things out back.

The Shark circled. Flew off down the coastline cloaked in clouds. A few minutes later, it came back roaring, stirring up the peace. The persistent droning of the plane running back and forth overhead, sounding as if it were on top of the house, wore on the nerves like a type of torture. The firefly-like ember under the mango tree went out, crushed to death by Konjah Man's thumb against his middle finger.

Konjah Man stood up, shouted praises to His Imperial Majesty, bun down Babylon, and got ready to push off to his next stop. He never stayed long when Judah wasn't home. Never said a lot. But somehow, he always seemed to know just how much of himself was needed to make wrong things right.

Inside the house, the grumbling of Nubya's phone vibrating against the countertop brought her back to the reality of the kitchen table with the bowls of sap growing cold in her possession. The sight of Judah's name on the display lifted her.

"Hey." The sweetness of her voice seeped out onto the device.

"All is well?" Judah queried. He could hear the Shark's engines grumbling in the background.

"Yeah. You?" She searched his voice for signs of distress. Strained to listen to his background sounds for clues of where he might be.

"Yeah," he replied, followed by a guttural sound that always put her at ease. The lion's purr, she called it.

"I soon come forward, so just relax. Everything bless." Judah knew how to answer her silent questions.

"I hear you," she submitted.

He clicked out. She finished her sap, waited a while in front of the muted TV. After which, Nubya unsuccessfully turned to the musty pages of a partially read book of selected speeches by Dr. Eric Williams that she had long been fighting to complete. When the restlessness came again, she went out onto the veranda and deeply inhaled the salty sea breeze. When she could wait no more, she dozed off in the front house hammock to the important sounding voices on BBC.

Nubya awoke to a feather-light kiss puckered on her forehead. Judah's smokey breath, spiced with the scent of a fermented brew, searched for her mouth. His lips hot on the trail. Sucking her in. She savored the sweet relief of his return home and pulled herself into his warmth.

TWO SEVENS

"It's another beautiful morning here in BLAZE-HD 98.3FM country, and you are sharing it with myself, the unforgettable Lady Khando, along with my ace of spades, DJ Kutlass. At the top of the hour, we ride into the mid-morning with Audio Provisions, brought to you by Vital—'For the Best Ital.'

"Before we change gears though, we have one more giveaway to make this morning. A pair of V.I.P. tickets to the upcoming Heroes Day show with headliners, Sizzla, Chronixx, and for the first time in Barbados, legends of reggae, Culture," Khando teased.

"Kutlass, is this real?" Lady Khando asked animatedly as she turned in the direction of the radio DJ.

"Yes, mi lady," he flirted. "Reggae royalty will be in the land next Saturday." Kutlass's reply came with a slight inflection of a Guyanese accent that caused his words to dance into the microphone. "Show promoter RAS Entertainment, the Revolutionary Action Syndicate, is calling this the godfather of all shows," Kutlass went on, hyping the event.

"Picture it. One night, one massive stage, three generations of reggae music's most heartical artists. To top it off, Culture is currently celebrating the fortieth anniversary of their iconic release of the *Two Sevens Clash* album," the morning DJ explained.

Khando replied, playing off of Kutlass's enthusiasm, "This is a big one! Barbados will never experience anything like this again. There's nowhere else to be for a show this massive, this historic, other than front and center, soaking up the sweet, conscious vibes."

"Hear what people, tickets have to give away." DJ Kutlass put on his serious tone as the music bed changed to a different reggae roots riddim.

"It's true," Khando squared up to him. "Now, these are no ordinary tickets we have here. These are two V.I.P. tickets of V.I.P. value. So, I promise you, this question will not be easy. But the reward for getting it right will definitely be sweet. The tickets will go to the caller who can tell us what happened when the two sevens clashed in 1977, and where did it all go down?"

Pushing away from his microphone as if the question was too hot for him, Kutlass exclaimed, "Whoa! That's a big one right there!" Then, in an assuring tone, he leaned into the microphone. "But I'm confident that our listeners are going to be all over it! The phone lines are lighting up already. We're going to start taking answers from our seventh caller on. The question again, 'What happened when the two sevens clashed in 1977, and where did it all go down?' Answer correctly and this pair of V.I.P. tickets is yours."

"Now this is all happening at the newly renovated, or should I say rebuilt, National Stadium?" Khando switched up the conversation and Kutlass ran with it.

"I guess it depends on how you choose to look at it. My thing is that shows haven't been held at that venue since, cha! ... It's been so long, I can't even remember how long it's been," Kutlass confessed.

"We should make that a question," Lady Khando instigated. "Like, who can tell us when the last show held at the National Stadium was?"

"Well, the correct answer would be, nuff years!" Kutlass chopped in, delivering the punchline with a nearly perfect Bajan accent.

"Have you seen it since it reopened last month?" Khando queried.

"Yeah, and I'll be there on Saturday, April twenty-eighth, when the *Two Sevens Clash* to bless up the show," DJ Kutlass confirmed.

Staying on topic, Khando continued, "I'm partially impressed, though. Never thought that our government would have ever recovered the missing dollars from the Sports Fund. Then on top of that, in record time, manage to make this new facility the reality it should have been like ever since."

"My research thus far shows that this is the first time lost monies of that magnitude, or of any size, have ever been recovered, thanks to a forensic audit. For a lottery-playing country like ours, it was truly puzzling how pop-down the stadium had become, especially when so much lotto money flows in every day in the name of sports, youth, and culture.

How could things like basic facility upkeep go unaddressed for so long?"

Khando dug further into the topic. "You know many aspiring youths with budding sports-related careers and so much potential got messed up because there was no proper training facility for them to hone their skills. On one hand, the government is out there promoting a message of support for our youth; yet, in these modern times, they left our nation's future athletes without a proper sporting facility for so long."

Kutlass joined in. "Thing is, a national stadium not only helps us with the development of our young people. There is also the tourism initiative, especially with sports tourism coming in as a close second in terms of being a foreign exchange earner after ecotourism. There is a demand for a state-of-the-art facility like this. It's coming from regional and international sports clubs and institutions and organizations looking for a place in the sun to train or hold events in a quality space. Meanwhile, we're over here snoozing on an opportunity."

"Shining bright like midnight," Lady Khando summed up.

"Just this morning, I drove by because I had to make a stop that took me in that direction," Kutlass contributed. "There's no denying that there is quite a sizable wow factor that the new stadium evokes."

"It's true!" Khando responded as she returned to her bubbly radio announcer mode.

DJ Kutlass began to wrap up the segment. "Barbados people, we are giving away two tickets! You heard right. For you and a special someone to be front row, backstage, and all points in between at the upcoming *Two Sevens Clash* massive reggae show next Saturday, Heroes' Day at the National Stadium. Be the seventh caller to correctly tell us about the legend of the *Two Sevens Clash* to win a pair of V.I.P. tickets to the show." DJ Kutlass's words segued into Lady Khando's call to action.

"Phone lines are open. The number to call is two-four-B-L-A-Z-E. In the meantime, from Sizzla's seventieth, you heard me right, his seventieth album, titled *The Messiah*, here is "Dem Nuh Business." I'm Lady Khando, riding shotgun with DJ Kutlass on BLAZE-HD 98.3FM. Music. Message. Forward."

The red "On Air" sign inside the studio had barely gone out before the off-air conversation took over the room. Zoe, the intern, was busy sifting through the social media chatter on her tablet.

"I bet you everybody's now looking up the answer," DJ Kutlass remarked with a half chuckle, lowering his headphones to his shoulder where they cupped his neck. He scanned through the playlist on the screen in front of him.

"I know, right," Lady Khando replied, her mind partially sidetracked. She had been on shaky ground with the station's management, specifically with the program director, ever since she'd taken over DJ Tangy's morning spot.

Tangy had jumped ship with little notice, breaking her contract for a better paying gig on some new station that popped up out of nowhere. They had the budget to haul in big-name personalities to play an influential role in their branding efforts. BLAZE's knee-jerk reaction to the fiasco resulted in all the shows that followed Tangy's being shifted forward a time slot, which moved Lady Khando from the late-night slot that she'd dominated for so long to the coveted five a.m. to ten a.m. spot Tangy vacated.

In one, Lady Khando birthed a whole new persona. She rebranded the previously mindless morning-time babble that came to define Tangy's popular show and replaced it with an edgy fete of savvy musical selections, interlaced with provocative, intelligent conversation. Somehow, management seemed more sour than happy than one would have expected, even though the listenership had increased, and two new segment sponsors came on board.

"Hey, don't forget you're playing at the opening tonight," Khando reminded Kutlass as she updated the show's log.

"What's the vibe for tonight?" Kutlass asked as he cued up the next song.

"Do you." Khando smiled. "That's what I want."

"I've got a correct answer here on the chat," Zoe interjected.

Lady Khando turned her attention to Zoe while she addressed the room. "Thirty seconds before we go live," she announced. "Kutlass, we'll go straight to the phone lines to see if we get the correct answer. If nothing comes in, we'll announce the winner from the messenger posts. Zoe, head down to reception and bring up our guests, so we can get the next promotional hour going."

The remainder of the morning was upbeat. Steve, the program director, was off island, which made being at the station feel lighter. After recording some voiceovers, Lady Khando tackled a queue of administrative tasks, then headed over to her Warrenstown gallery to prepare for the evening's opening reception.

Driving northbound, away from the capital, along the

coastal highway, Lady Khando let her mind wander as it always did when she drove along that stretch of road. Her thoughts rested on how, in a short space of time, what was once acres of bush had morphed into Warrenstown—a burgeoning eco-metropolis of stunted high rises that poked at the belly of the sky above it.

Lady Khando's family owned a small piece of real estate that straddled the border of Warrenstown and the suburb of Welches Terrace, along the northeastern strip of the ABC Highway. The sleek seven-story, mid-century, modern-styled building gleamed with importance.

How Khando's father sensed that the spot of rab land he had inherited should house luxury high-rise units, or where he gathered the tenacity to ride that dream into reality, remained a thing of legend. No matter the angle the story was told from, it always proved utterly pioneering.

Local banks, adamant that Khando's father's construction project was overly ambitious, were reluctant to fund it. In that time, as it was now, post-independence Barbados turned its attention to pimping its natural resources to lure British and North American tourists to its tropical shores, en masse.

Centuries of doctrine had affirmed that the island's soil was too shallow and nutrient deficient to competitively support agriculture, except when it came to growing sugar cane. The islanders had been told that the only economic footing they could have in the world was as a raw materials producer. Over time, that proved unsuccessful, given the law of economies of scale that weighed against the tiny isle.

When sugar was king, the production of sugar was handled by a collective of thousands of islanders who, for centuries, received no compensation for their labor. Now things had changed. With paid labor a reality, somehow, the sugar industry found it hard to exist as the lucrative foreign exchange earner it used to be.

Someone of influence whispered "tourism" into the right decision makers' ears as the saving grace for the people of the land. Just like that, it was so.

Tourism was touted as the cure to sustain the country's at-risk financial health brought on by the sugar industry's waning ability to compete on the global market. The prophecy was clear: Foreign exchange was necessary if one wanted to purchase foreign goods, which, it was rumored, were far superior to those produced locally and so should be desired.

Barbados lured tourists from developed nations to the island. Those tourists brought with them their sought-after foreign currency when they visited. In its rhetorical form, tourism seemed promising, offering up sun, sea, sand, and friendly people as a recipe for a good time in exchange for much needed foreign currency. Why else would tourism really matter?

So, every day for weeks, months, years, and decades since that first whisper, islanders labored at promoting their attractive destination to people from not-so-attractive places. The pundits, however, had a myopic take on tourism, which boxed it into a corral of limitations.

The thought of building a condominium farther than a few feet from a beach was seen as ludicrous. Surely, travelers to the island wanted the postcard experience of sun-drenched beaches lined with coconut palm trees. Though that may have been true for the typical visitor, Mr. Cadogan, being an ideas man, saw things differently.

"Welcome to Cadogan Towers, Ms. Cadogan." An attentive valet delivered the greeting as Khando's Jeep Wrangler Unlimited swooped in, coming to a stop in the porte-cochère at the main entrance to the building. He swiftly opened the driver's side door as she popped out of the vehicle, simultaneously gathering her belongings from the front passenger seat.

Cadogan Towers was luxury living. Concierge service, gym, pool, spa, gallery, meeting space, a boutique, a realtor office, and the tony Kasa Mansa Restaurant and Rooftop Bar, with its contemporary take on Senegalese and North African cuisine.

"I would have called in to try and win those tickets this morning, but you got me with that question," the valet confessed.

"Well, I still have more tickets to give away. You still have a week to try to answer my questions correctly." Khando smiled smartly and proceeded into the sprawling reception area.

"I'm not giving up," he called after her as he chuckled to himself. If it were anyone else, he may have risked it and asked for free tickets. But Lady Khando's reputation preceded her. She was not a fan of hobby-class people on the lookout for freebies.

The impressiveness of Cadogan Towers dripped from every detail. The architect had been requested to employ design techniques that directed the trade winds throughout the entire ground-floor lobby area. Exotic palm trees and broadleaf philodendrons adorned the reception area, which seamlessly spilled out onto a courtyard punctuated by a centralized water feature in the midst of a cozy seating space.

Cadogan Towers was a West Indian interpretation of an undeniable South Beach Miami vibe. Its play on muted colors, geometric patterns, and lush landscaping oozed Caribbean chic. Swirling with tropical faces, upon entering the lobby of the towers, one immediately felt transported, important, and welcomed all at the same time.

Requisite greetings aside, Lady Khando made her way to the east-end space that housed her art gallery. The Reuben Gallery was her joy. Approaching the glass-walled space, the artwork for the opening exhibition seemed to leap out from the inside. Roused with excitement, she quickened her pace.

"Oh, this is striking!" she exclaimed upon entering the gallery to take a closer look at the finished layout. It wasn't her first exhibition, but each one always evoked a feeling of elation.

"Good afternoon, Marley," her assistant, Zenobia, greeted her, rising from an alcove near the entrance. "All of the pieces are up. Duti just left. Said not to worry. He will make sure to be back before the starting time. The caterers will be here shortly to set up. I've followed up with the art buyers, media houses, and bloggers; everyone will be in attendance. Mr. Cadogan stopped by to take a peek at the exhibit," she concluded matter-of-factly.

"Perfect! Good afternoon to you, as well," Marley replied, satisfied with the update. "Sounds like we are set for tonight."

"Oh, yeah, one more thing," her assistant added, jump-starting a new conversation. "*Two Sevens Clash*. That was the name of Culture's first album, which came out on the seventh of July 1977. In the title song, a prediction had been made about when the two sevens clash. There are two sevens in 1977 and the seventh of July. July being the seventh month is another set of sevens. There was so much hype and bad predictions about the date that Jamaican schools and businesses closed down on July 7, 1977 as a precaution."

Pleased, Marley smiled broadly, taking in the sharpness of her assistant. Marley glided into the back office and took her place at the helm of her desk. Perched on the threshold of the office door, a mischievous grin stayed plastered on Zenobia's face as she continued.

"I would have called in to win those tickets. But then you would have thought I was slacking on the job," she teased. "We all know that Mademoiselle Marley Cadogan is not having that. So I'll just wait for those comp tickets that you know I'm dying to get, which you've already set aside for me. Correct is right. Right, Lady Khando?" Zenobia jokingly petitioned in a pseudo Caribbean-sounding accent that Marley could never place.

Animatedly, Zenobia winked at Marley and returned to the reception desk, leaving behind chuckles of disbelief from her boss.

3

THE PENTHOUSE

Marley hadn't left Duti's side for a moment. Guiding him through the maze of awe-filled faces cocked at varying degrees of interest, Duti Boukman, the man of the evening, passionately answered questions, giving insight into the sea of mysteries that gripped the audience. The press lapped up the juiciness attributed to Marley's association with the artist widely rumored to be a practicing Obeah Man.

The quirky nature of Marley's exhibitions always carried a strange appeal, which was heightened by her status as a socialite media personality. That aside, her success in bridging the gap between the artistic realm and popular culture was undisputed.

A few months earlier, Marley backed an exhibition of dub posters curated by Zenobia, who had approached her with the idea. It seemed basic, showcasing a selection of street promotion posters from dub sessions of the past decade, which were pulled from the archives of three of the island's most prolific counterculture graphic artists.

Unexpectedly, the launch turned into an impromptu dub session itself. The opening night, however, wasn't at Marley's space, The Reuben Gallery in Cadogan Towers, nor its sister gallery at the nearby UWI campus, where complementing installations of the exhibition hung. This toss, the opening was held at a venue that, years prior, had housed the legendary Penthouse nightclub, a former mecca for dub sessions at the height of its story. It only stood to reason that Marley would repurpose the iconic spot into a pop-up gallery as a shrine to the essence of dub culture.

Long retired from its partying days, the Penthouse was like a polished gem stashed away in a forgotten jewelry box. The second-floor walk-up, with its clean walls and refurbished hardwood floors, was loft-like in appearance.

Climbing the narrow stairway, a few steps through the threshold revealed the spaciousness of the building. The bar area and the dance floor looked game to try a little something. Across from them, a pair of doors opened onto the lone balcony and sole alternative exit out of the club. There was no fire escape—just faith that one would be alright if something were to ever go wrong.

The view from the Penthouse was rich. The street below bustled with the hustle of city life flowing through it. Vendors and pedestrians ruled the two sizable public markets at either end of the area. A cluster of rum shops was precariously situated like a roundabout, standing in the middle of the intersection, where three arteries of roads converged. Everything poured into and circulated around the drink and food vendors that traded from those stalls, bordered by taxi men leaning against their parked vehicles, passing the time by playing dominoes.

There was Marhill Street in the east, populated with fast-food restaurants and horse racing betting circuits. There was also a narrow side road that led from Broad Street in the west, winding its way past a large commercial bank, then wrapping around a parking garage that sat diagonally across from the Parliament building. All linked up with the northbound road that curved eastward to Roebuck Street, bypassing the police headquarters.

A stretch of roadside clothing boutiques flashed the latest in urban wear outside their storefronts, which carried elaborate setups of draped clothing swinging in the open air, with the hope of enticing passersby. From the balcony of the Penthouse, one could see it all.

The bar was on crank. The exhibition opening was presided over by a popular dub music selector, who incorporated the event into his weekly online live broadcast show. Everyone came out that night. Gathered on the sidewalk, well ahead of the start time, pools of guests began to form.

What brought the people out in numbers was anyone's guess. The energy governing the exhibition itself was a weird concoction of high society, ghetto culture, and artsy fartsy vibes. No one knew what to expect.

Marley had secured a loud music permit to facilitate the music element of the opening. But she hadn't foreseen a need to request permission for temporary road closure for the stretch in front of the club. It just wasn't that deep.

The numbers who came out, though, exceeded the hundred or so invitees who were expected to trickle in at various intervals of the night. Soon enough, the road below was clogged with bodies. The lone entrance in and out of the

Penthouse made the ushers work overtime to man the gallery traffic. Below, those waiting to view the exhibition limed and partied along the curb as the music wafted outdoors from the powerful house speaker system.

If you've ever been to the Penthouse in its heyday, reggae dancehall dub riddims weren't the only thing that wafted out from the balcony above. In the nostalgia of the moment, hidden in the thick of things, someone, somewhere sparked up. When the natural mystic mingled in with the night's proceedings, it was quietly acknowledged that the opening had taken on the spirit of dub sessions past.

On the balcony of the Penthouse, an oversized banner designed in dub poster style draped from the building, announcing the exhibition. The call-in programs were in a tizzy the next day, when it was reported that the artwork was quite obscene, with poster vixens posing in less than desirable positions under a saucy headline. Nothing new, it was a discussion that was brewing from the first time the banner was mounted just days earlier.

Marley was accused of being able to get away with whatever she wanted "in this fair land" because of connections. A few callers commented with disdain on how "people" were in the street smoking herb just a few feet away from the police headquarters. Old rhetoric about guns and violence, obscenity and noise pollution, flowed in between mentions of young persons' blatant disregard for the citizens of Barbados.

There were lamentations on how a street was closed down in the middle of town on a Wednesday night to accommodate foolishness. The few conversations about the art stripped the exhibition of its cultural relevance until

Marley called into the programs herself in an attempt to refocus the discussions.

On social media, some artists swore blind that Marley carried things too far and needed to realize that ruffling feathers was not good for other artists' livelihoods. She should try to operate with more care, as her actions negatively impacted other artists devoid of a silver spoon. The streets, of course, shrugged at the spectacle of a dub poster being elevated to the status of some kind of art.

"Money people don't have nothing more to do than this sorta ting," or responses like, "But wait ... that is Man Features' picture on da poster 'cross dey?" ended up being talking points for the everyday person. All talk aside, the session—or was it an opening—did what Marley quietly knew it would do: insight dialogue, sell art, and make life spicy.

Marley magnified Duti's shine. Theirs was a latent closeness that danced to its own tune, in its own space, without stepping into the realm of the real world. As an artist plying his trade of employing art as a medium of an abstract recital of the lore of mystic men of Obeah, Duti wore the raiment well. A visual mystery, the topography of his face, illuminated by the presence of an ancient wisdom suspended in a youthful energy, was spellbinding.

Duti had long studied the science of Obeah—its practices and its criminality. Lived it, too. He had met Marley by chance at Miami International Airport while in transit to Barbados. Immediately recognizing him in the waiting area, she had gone over and introduced herself to the much talked about high priest. He was iconic, with a rock-star status, seldom associated with one so grounded. A flight delay extended the introductory exchange into a full conversation.

It took two years for it all to come together. In that time, Duti the artist became Duti the friend. Now he was here, touring his exhibition and coffee table book through the Caribbean, with next steps taking him to Nairobi, Kenya.

Spirits in wine glasses intoxicated guests while DJ Kutlass bewitched the patrons musically. The exhibition set out to align current reality with ancient mysteries of yesteryear that lurked in the curious corners of modern-day imaginings.

The mandate of The Reuben Gallery was simple: Reshape what was accepted as art on the home front. Marley had long grown tired of the bondage perpetuated by the chattel house and donkey cart imagery as representative of a people who, at heart, were void of the romantic sentiments being touted as heritage. The limitations of that conversation denied visual artists the leverage to be boundless in their expression, unshackled from imperialist dictates on identity and message.

"In your element."

Marley looked up at the sound of her father's deep voice reaching out toward her upon his approach. A blogger had just snatched Duti away for an interview.

"Cadogan." She smiled at him. "I heard you came peeking about the place earlier. What have I told you about doing that?" Marley teased, leaning into her father's embrace.

"Well, your mother asked me to send her some photos before things got too busy. So I obliged," Mr. Cadogan responded, used to his recurring role as peacemaker.

"I don't know why she bothers," Marley retorted, the sunniness temporarily leaving her face. Mrs. Cadogan was a free spirit, with little time for anything other than what interested her. She lived life passionately, loving everything, being present for everyone, but somehow remaining absent in Marley's story.

"Marley," Mr. Cadogan pleaded quietly, acutely aware of the crowd, the cameras ... the need for his daughter to shine on her night. "Don't be that way."

"Have you met the artist, Duti Boukman?" Marley served, redirecting the conversation as she scanned the room for his light while she rekindled hers.

"Should I meet him?" Mr. Cadogan teased. "I'm not sure how I feel about all this mystic mumbo jumbo you have going on here or if I want to meet this so-called high priest artist."

"Here is something that would interest you. Have you seen the number of red dots next to Mr. Mystic Mumbo Jumbo's work?" Marley challenged.

"It's hard not to notice them. They are quite plentiful," her father admitted. "I take it then, that congratulations are in order for another successful opening?"

"If you insist. Just don't let it be said that I coerced it out of you," Marley teased as she interlocked her arm with Mr. Cadogan's and directed him across the room to the place where Duti stood.

4

BAM BAM

A small afterparty made its way to Marley's suite, a modest two-bedroom, split-level condo on the fifth floor of Cadogan Towers. Marley's home was brochure perfect, with a wrap-around wall of windows, high ceilings, and an open floor plan, complete with an intimately sized terrace that extended the living and dining spaces onto the outdoors.

Glasses of wine flavored the pockets of conversations that dotted Marley's residence. DJ Kutlass uploaded a few mixes to the surround sound system and set the mood to a Rocksteady/Studio One vibe that was conversation friendly yet loud enough to motivate a pair of Marley's guests to start dancing. The energy was nice.

Though rare, given her hectic schedule, gatherings at Marley's home were like havens for souls to temporarily unveil themselves in the sanctuary of her space, poised high above the status quo.

Marley heard the door to the foyer open. I-Am stepped off the condo's private elevator, with her brother Shotta

Forward and his brother Zaire in tow, and made her way to the living room area, with its stunning view of Warrenstown stretched out beyond it. Like any true bona fide who has a key to their friend's spot, I-Am had the access code to Marley's private elevator.

"You made it!" Marley sang out, approaching them with arms wide open. She extended a warm welcome to all before they could fully enter the room.

"Sis, yuh done know," Shotta Forward responded warmly.

The living room sat on one side of the open plan, while the kitchen and dining room were on the other. Shotta Forward made his rounds, hailing up a few people he knew, including Kutlass, who was sitting across from Duti at the dining table, engrossed in conversation. Marley returned to the sectional that she and Zenobia were hogging up previously. She retracted her body into a comfortable coil as she invited her guests to sit with her.

"I know you're always saying that I don't visit you enough," Shotta Forward said apologetically as he took a seat on the adjacent couch of the sectional with timid familiarity. Though Marley was welcoming, Shotta Forward always seemed hesitant to relax in the comfort of her friendship. It was a familiar story that led many to address her with the respect reserved for the privileged.

Such rigid structures were the domain of the unspoken. Marley had inherited her family's legacy, and no matter what fold of society she found herself wrapped in, the unspoken always led the way, even in basic everyday interactions.

"Whenever you get here is the right time to be here, so no worries." Marley shrugged off Shotta's concern as she scoped out the panoramic view of the sprawl of Warrenstown.

Although the metropolis of artificial lights muted the opulence of the plump moon's rays pouring down from a navy blue Caribbean sky, the man-made splendor viewed from the condo's vantage point was undeniable.

"I have a spread that I know you are going to like," Marley offered eagerly as she rose to make her way across to the kitchen, catching the attention of her friend and personal chef, Rita, who had just finished plating a platter with canapes.

"Forward, you know I get nervous whenever you come over." A broad smile stretched across Shotta Forward's face as Rita, looking quite pleased with herself, contrary to her words, brought over two platters of assorted vegan tapas and rested them on the coffee table that was central to the group.

"Now, my Ital is not like your Ital. But it still can hold its own," Rita declared to Shotta Forward and Zaire, having gone down this road before, catering for Marley's guests.

"Tonight, I asked Rita to do a Creole-inspired something. Everything is excellent, but I'm especially liking the lentil-stuffed yam poppers, done in the way you're always suggesting: baked, not fried," Marley continued as she drew closer—returning from the kitchen with fingers interlocked between some flute glasses in one hand and two bottles of spirits in the other.

"Marley, yuh blessed! Yuh done know!" Shotta Forward replied, grateful for the care she always took to make sure that whenever he landed, he felt comfortable.

Marley was flanked by Zenobia and I-Am on either side. At opposing ends of the sectional rested Shotta and Zaire, who was busy chopping up a small stainless-steel bowl of Bajan Green. It seemed like a ritual that, whenever Shotta Forward arrived, the finest of Bajan Green would follow.

"What do you think?" Shotta Forward asked, leaning away from Marley as Zaire passed her the bowl of partially chopped herb. She ran an uncut bud under her nose, inhaling the aromatic fragrance of the fresh grade, then pinched it to yield the stickiness.

"Divine." She smiled, looking at Forward and I-Am, who nodded proudly in agreement. Zenobia popped open a bottle of champagne that Marley had handed to her earlier and began to fill three glasses. She poured Shotta Forward a cognac and Zaire, whose diet was strictly Ital based, refreshed with some coconut water. When the sharing was completed, Marley toasted her friends then gave Zenobia a look, which read more like a suggestion. It moved Zenobia to secure her champagne flute and bee-line it across the room to join Duti and DJ Kutlass at the dining table.

"A Vincy shot get lick up tonight," Shotta Forward revealed upon Zenobia's departure.

"Judah and Nubya were to be here all like now, but she messaged and said they weren't coming across anymore. Not sure what, if anything, happened," Marley shared.

"You see what I tell yuh? I trying to avoid that kind of action altogether and just focus on local," Shotta Forward informed. The obstacle course for calling a shot had gotten harder. Landing herb had become way too risky with the Shark overhead, coast guards in the sea, and gangsters on the ground.

"Yeah, but from what her message said, nothing major went wrong," Marley unloaded.

"Don't take this the wrong way. I don't think Shotta is saying anything against calling a shot because we know that dealing with homegrown ain't easy, either," I-Am continued, taking deep draws from a Vicks inhaler that seemed to be permanently lodged in her right nostril.

"Look, production is up. Like we really doing this," I-Am admitted. "With a good crop, we are getting like a grand off of one tree. But the only thing is that you have to carry the crop to time," she explained.

Shotta Forward then reasoned to the group, "We are looking for a property that we can take this whole operation to, because with this open crop action ... cha! Men stealing yuh weed ... Johnny Law raiding de place ... got yuh can't relax. Can't wait for the herb to mature so you can move on and make things happen."

No matter how Marley listened to the conversation, whether a man was calling an overseas shot or risking at local cultivation, someone was always breathing down the neck of the operation.

"Once we can be patient and let the plants grow fully, in a protected environment, we will see some nice returns on investment," I-Am assured.

I-Am had eight green fingers and two green thumbs. Once she touched anything, it bloomed. Many people were of the opinion that Shotta Forward was the one growing premium herb, which was true to an extent. But it was his sister's golden touch that seduced fat buds from their trees.

On the front end, Shotta Forward was a legitimate entrepreneur with his popular Ital shops, Vital and Vital Too. He was doing well enough that weekly he would host a sponsored Vital segment on Marley's morning show.

Shotta Forward was always inclined to Marley. As a child, he would come over to the Cadogans' on days that his mother couldn't help but to bring him to work at her job as the Cadogans' housekeeper. At age five, Shotta disappeared from Marley's life—until one teenage day, when they ran into each other at a friend's party. From then on, Shotta Forward made sure never to lose touch of Marley again.

She was different in a way he couldn't characterize. He was fond of her efforts of promoting a positive message on her morning radio show, as well as how gracious she naturally was.

Marley was dealt a winning hand. But after she once confessed that she was having problems at work, Shotta Forward (who was quite prone to having strong feelings) decided to buy an hour of time during her shift twice a week for an ongoing period. He did so in hopes that his sponsorship commitment would help sway management into seeing the value Marley brought, in a language they understood: *money*.

In her gratitude, she'd broadcast the occasional coded messages tucked inside of a shout-out that, when deconstructed, delivered valuable intel to the gatekeepers of the ghetto grapevine. Marley would talk hidden in plain sight, sweetened by some DJ hype, underscored with a themed song, which seemed harmless. However, to those in the know, the meaning was deeper.

In ritual form, the bowl made its rounds at the table while a similar bowl was making its rounds amongst the other guests. DJ Kutlass came over and gave thanks to Shotta Forward before heading outside to join up with Duti, who was now on the terrace with Zenobia and Rita.

"We want to diversify and expand, Marley," I-Am offered as she handed her a ganja-infused lollipop. "It's not our thing, but people like them. They are a hit with partygoers."

I-Am continued updating Marley, without waiting for her response on the lollipop. Despite an assortment of experiences with burning herb, personally, Marley remained a lover of the bong draw, a spillover from university days abroad. She had spent all night over her three-foot bong, burning Shotta Forward's Bajan Green, stopping periodically on her inhale to savor the umami flavor from the draw of herb.

Was it even a secret that Marley moved ganja products with the same sophistication that she masterfully sold art? Yes, and she wanted it to remain that way.

The stink of the high grade wafted out onto the terrace to be carried off by the late-night air. The evolution of ganja's uses was a constant talking point for Marley and I-Am. There was a desire to innovate and lead the market. But that had to be tempered with protecting the reverence due to herb as a holy sacrament.

I-Am and Marley's conversation gradually dissolved. DJ Kutlass blew back smoke like a prayer to the sky as he swayed with Zenobia, who was now dancing in his direction, backdropped by the glow of Warrenstown. I-Am, Zaire, and Rita ended up hashing it out in the kitchen. Shotta Forward made his way to the far end of the terrace, where he found himself in the company of a Dominican documentary filmmaker.

With each toke, Marley's home became increasingly alive. Duti came over and sat down, nestling alongside

Marley. The music had transitioned to an intergalactic Caribbean dub funk that transported them through a sonic galaxy of notes.

The last thing Marley remembered was stretching out over a stack of cushions, then burrowing her head into a comfortable spot on Duti's lap. She closed her eyes on the downbeat and woke up the next morning to a stunning silence.

5

OLD FYAH STICK EASY FI KETCH

The greater part of Saturday morning had gone before Marley finally got out of the house. Wednesday's exhibition opening and post-event soirée was followed by station duties the next couple of days, mixed with consecutive evenings of event hosting, which left her feeling fagged out when she awoke.

The day in front, Duti received an urgent request to go to Trinidad. Marley respected his privacy and didn't pry, although she suspected it was a political call. Duti respected Marley's work and wouldn't stop apologizing for leaving in the middle of his press commitments for his much-anticipated exhibition. He was authentically offset, but Marley cushioned his concerns by assuring him that she would reschedule his appearances. She then made him promise to give her one of his famed bush baths upon his return to Barbadian soil.

By the time she made it into the daylight, Saturday had unfolded with the sun in the afternoon position, throwing spears of heat toward the island. It had been too many months ago that she had been to the cemetery. When Marley awoke that morning, she knew that today would be the day to make the visit.

Marley abandoned her Jeep for the somewhat worn L200 she used on these occasions. She threw a tote bag of just-in-case clothes into the back seat before heading east. Masked by the growl of the engine, music from a recent promotion mixtape made its way to her ears ever so often, mostly coming to her attention when she shifted gears.

The afternoon was crisp. One of those clear days with a crystal-like quality that made everything sparkle in its own right. Nubya was calling. Marley hit the handsfree button.

"Hi, Bella Bella. How are you?" she sang out.

"Irie. you still coming up?"

"Yeah. I'm on my way now. Just have one stop to make."

"Alright. See you soon."

"Latas, Bella Bella."

Pulling into the churchyard, Marley parked in her usual spot by some mature frangipani trees. A few feet away, buried side by side in a beautifully adorned grave, lay her grandparents. The gravesite was far enough from the church to have privacy; yet, it was close enough to be honorable. It had been nearly a decade since the last Cadogan was laid to rest there.

The double gravesite resembled a miniature box garden with lush flowers contained within its painted border. The graveyard as a whole was well maintained, with a carpet of manicured grass bordering a canopy of trees. Interspersed throughout were all manner of headstones. Marley paid her respects, then sat in silence on the edge of the gravesite.

"Marley." The baritone resonance of the voice tingled.

She looked up at the familiar figure.

"Lee Mile?"

"Yes!"

They both laughed in excitement, silent memories exploding behind the astonished gaze of their locked eyes.

"How have you been?" she queried as the mood began to settle down.

"Keeping quiet," he replied. The graveyard came alive with conversation as their voices were pelted around by the jipsy wind that kept tangling up in their words.

It was an eternity of conversation that betrayed the fact that they both lived on the same small island. Not seeing each other for so long couldn't have been so hard. But it happened. Lee Mile smiled down at her. The words continued to flow. At one point, he squatted down to fork up a small corner of the flower bed with the tip of his machete.

"I see your father more than I see you," he offered.

"Yeah?" Marley responded.

Lee Mile was a younger man to Marley's father and an older man to her. Roughly ten years her senior.

"Cadogans in St. Andrew," he mused. "Thought Cadogans were from St. Lucy."

"We are, but my grandparents fell in love with St. Andrew, so much so that they made it their wish to be buried in this parish. Well, more like they bought their burial spots here and the family had to comply." A smirk formed on her face as the memory ran through her mind. "Things are so different now, when you think of it," Marley continued, looking across at Lee Mile. "We live, for the most part, in Warrenstown. Gran-Gran and Grandfather are buried out here in the country, way behind God's back. Our St. Lucy life is now about visiting family or checking in on land. We don't really actively do anything down there.

"Some people say we've gotten rich and switched ..." Marley almost looked as if she was seriously pondering what people were saying about her family, "which is silly 'cause we've always had money."

They talked until just before sundown, when the streetlights came on and members of the church choir filtered in for practice. The sky was a gradient of monochromatic blue that transitioned from a glowing powdery hue in the west, to a blue-black onyx in the east. Night was approaching. Underneath the emerging stars, they stood.

"We have been fortunate to witness the passing of another day," Lee Mile concluded as they made their way to the car park. Packing his tools into his truck, Lee Mile looked across at Marley. "Tonight, I dance with my Orisha. You are most welcome to join me," he offered.

As a young girl, Marley had always heard that Lee Mile came from a family of mystics. It was just that no one ever said it so prettily. He appeared to be no stranger than her aunt, who counted backwards from ten to one if she'd left home and abruptly had to turn around to retrieve whatever she had forgotten. Or Marley's cousin, who wore two crystals, one for protection, and the other for repelling negative energy, each tucked securely under her tiny popped-down breasts. Even when Gran-Gran was alive, she would tap the ground twice with her wooden walking stick if she dared to tempt fate by stating aloud a perceived outmaneuvering of a possible mishap.

Lee Mile knew the bush well enough to heal others with bush remedies. In these times, that had a way of making people think one was up to something otherworldly. Especially people who had grown away from tradition, preferring prescription medication to treat everything from their children's lack of upbringing to their husband's loss of desire in bed. On the surface though, it was widely accepted that he was a farmer.

The village of Bawdens, where Lee Mile lived, was less than a quarter of a mile away from the parish church. Here, the government ran their Land for Lease initiative. Not as widely known was that most of the area not under government jurisdiction belonged to Lee Mile's family.

Lee Mile's nine siblings showed no interest in the land, but he did. On his orchard grew local cashew, guava, gooseberry, grapefruit, lime, Bajan cherry, jamoon, five fingers, sour soup, mango, and coconut. The fallow areas not in production were covered in a pasture that was harvested for hay.

Central to it all was a huge pond that sat quietly behind a patch of shrubbery, tucked away behind the abodes of families-cum-neighbors. It was the only aboveground manifestation of the extensive water supply that ran beneath in a maze of underground springs for acres on end.

Turning off of the main road, Marley followed Lee Mile down a dusty gap. He swung onto a track that ran between two rows of houses, which led onto a backroad-type area where an approaching "Y" in the road split the gap.

He veered left and drove into what appeared to be a wilderness. Then, Lee Mile rounded a corner that led into a clearing, on which sat a property entrance marked by two towering casuarina trees, where his portion of the family land began.

His soft stone house rested alert on the landscaped grounds. A mosaic treatment of gravel and steppingstones interwoven with scrunchineel, maypole, aloe, and other succulents gave the area a clean, unencumbered feel. Long rows of cuscus grass created a border-defining hedge where the landscape required it.

Lee Mile lived as he pleased. The house was small by all accounts, but the property around it seemed endless. Las Estrellas, he had named it.

The bright light of the final glow of sunset washed across the corralled expanse, revealing a pair of horses standing in the distance on the field. Pressed against the horizon of the eastern skyline were the faint outlines of sand dunes in the distance.

Leaving two of his workmen to unpack his truck, Lee Mile and Marley headed up the side steps that led into the dining area. People were already at the house when they arrived, many of them family from nearby.

"You still know how to live," Marley confessed softly as they made their way to the kitchen.

Smiling back, Lee Mile presented Marley with some drink choices, then proceeded to instruct the slender young lady, a cousin or niece, who was pouring coconut milk into a buck pot of ground provisions, to be sure to attend to Marley while he got cleaned up.

All of the years she had known Lee Mile, his abode always captivated her. The way it opened unto a generous wooden deck that ushered in the expanse of the backyard. The postcard-type view resembling ranch-styled, tropical, rustic frontier living, accented by a celestial canvas of stars. Scanning the span of the night's sky, it felt like Lee Mile lived in the thick of them.

The slender girl fondly remembered Marley from before. She reminded Marley of their last meeting, then returned to saying little while doing much. Out in the backyard, a small bonfire was dancing in the distance. Some musicians were half-tuning instruments, half-playing pieces of songs. Marley had settled in on a deck chair to eat when a loud-sounding car horn abruptly stopped the drifting thoughts of her mind.

"Lee Mile, I am paunched." Marley retired her spoon into the mostly empty calabash bowl, resting the pair on the tree trunk fashioned into a side table next to her. Lee Mile smiled, having returned happy that he had made sure she ate while he got changed.

"Did you taste the shaddon beni?"

"Which herb was that? The one that tastes like 'Come Tuh Muh?'" she taunted.

"No," he cracked at the ludicrousness of the joke as he took a seat in the chair next to her. Come Tuh Muh was a fabled potion that lovers added to dishes to make their true love remain interested ... or was it *faithful?*

"The one that tastes like cilantro."

"Oh, it wasn't cilantro?" she mused. "Nice, though."

The drumming was shaping up, along with the chants that recited folklore-old songs sung in a foreign tongue.

"Where did you disappear to this time?" The brief silence between them ushered in the storm.

"Why? Did you miss me?" Lee Mile responded jokingly.

"Yes. I did." The pointedness of her reply made Lee Mile rethink his response.

"It's fine," he assured.

"For you. Not for me. It's so bittersweet. It stings."

"The bitter is the healing." His words landed comfortingly on her shoulders, only to be shaken off by a thunderous voice that burst onto the scene, causing all within earshot to look up.

"Heeeey, Baba! Na nga def!" The words rolled ahead of the extended long, gangly arms that instantly embraced Lee Mile's defined shoulders. A hearty hug accentuated by pats on the back was topped off with an endearing toothy smile.

"Maa ngi fi rekk! Ahhhh! Mon frère! I heard you were back!" Lee Mile's reply matched the greeter's exuberance. Lee Mile grinned with delight, happy to see his guest.

"Your people at the market?" the guest queried.

"They are not my only source!" Lee Mile reminded his guest. Before more could be said on the subject, Lee Mile launched into a fresh set of pleasantries. "Papa Hanne, allow me to present to you my wife, Marley."

Lee Mile's introduction caused Marley to blush. Inwardly offset, her mind raced. How dare Lee Mile lay claim to her in that way? It always vexed her when he did that.

She had met this guest once before at an event at Kasa Manse, the Senegalese restaurant on the rooftop of Cadogan Towers. Was he the new owner? It was rumored he was the son or some relative to the previous owner. Smooth. Confident. Radiant. Marley hadn't yet got his full story.

"Hello, Hanne. Nice to meet you." She forced a genuine smile.

"Papa."

"Pardon?"

"Papa is my name, not a title," he explained in the richest of French West African accents.

"Okay. Hello, Papa," Marley repeated the correction. "Nice to meet you."

"Enchantée."

Turning his attention back to Lee Mile, he said, "Breddah, seriously, the daughter of Monsieur Cadogan is your wife?" Papa queried in pretend disbelief as Marley made note that he knew who she was.

"What are you trying to say? A man such as myself is not deserving of the sweetness of life?" Lee Mile chided.

"No, no, no. It's just that, now, I must respect you even more. I've seen Madame Marley at the Towers, with her smile as brilliant as a tropical sunset. Now come to find out that your courage is greater than mine and she is yours!"

"You seem not to know that I have royal courage. That I am a descendant of a king," Lee Mile proclaimed half-jokingly.

"Ha! A dream of yours," Papa speculated.

"No, I only speak the truth. You remember King Jaja of Opobo, Nigeria?" Lee Mile protested, launching into the first few lines of the Bajan folk song, "King Jaja." "I am his great, great, grand something. That's my claim!"

They all laughed. Marley, against her will.

"Your gallery is exquisite." Papa directed the compliment with sincerity toward Marley. "The exhibition that is there! Breddah, what do you think of it?"

"I haven't seen it as of yet. I only just returned a few days ago, myself. Marley?"

Marley decided to remain a quiet observer to the

exchange between her supposed husband and his guest. Hanne quickly cooked up a proposal.

"Have your wife give you a tour this week coming. Then, the two of you should stop by for dinner afterward. I have a new chef. I want you to, as you say, taste his hand. He's from St. Louis. He is a visionary in his representation of traditional Senegalese fare. Simply magnifique."

Lee Mile smoothly circumvented the offer. "What are we drinking tonight?" he asked, surveying his immediate circle of friends.

"Palm wine!" Papa declared.

"I have brought this crate especially for you. This here," Papa instructed, having produced a bottle separate from the gift he'd just presented to Lee Mile, "we partake of now."

Magically, three glasses appeared as if by sleight of hand. Papa opened the bottle and handed out partially filled drinking vessels to each of them. Lee Mile tipped his glass, pouring some of his wine onto the ground next to his sandaled foot, then raised a toast to his friends. "May the ancestors dance with us tonight. Salut!"

"À votre santé!"

"Cheers!"

6

CHA!

Two glasses in, it dawned on Marley that she hadn't left home to be with Lee Mile. He had that way about him—one which hijacked her attention, making her forget to remember. But not this time. Lee Mile was still close by, but the music was beginning to have its effect on him.

Pulling out her phone, Marley's heart sank at the sudden realization that she was in a dead zone. The night was still fresh, but it was night. Her people were waiting, and she was late. Looking over at Lee Mile, Marley mused at his strong, defined arms affixed to his statuesque frame, which was borne up by long, slightly bowed legs. His clean skin glowed under a thin layer of herb-infused shea butter, accented with a hint of khus oil, which he had extracted from the root of the cuscus grass.

Lee Mile smelled as good as he looked, and he never looked bad a day in his life. Marley knew that if she didn't leave now, her weekend would be ruined, hours discarded in passionate discourse. She was not in that place, mentally or otherwise.

Her thoughts reached him. Sensing she was ready to leave, he approached her. Marley smiled the way she did before disarming a situation, but there was no need for it here. He had already felt the shift in her energy. It was now a matter of her physically going.

"Are you ready?" Lee Mile asked, taking in the fullness of her countenance.

"Yes."

"Let me walk you to your truck," he offered.

"Give thanks."

They slid outside, walking in silence. Lee Mile was respectfully close behind, observing her gait. The yard light from his house cast their shadows ahead of them.

The night was nippy. The St. Andrew east coast breeze was slightly colder than equatorial chilly. Its bite caused Marley to shiver in the spaghetti-strapped, shin-long maxi dress she had donned in response to the roaring sun from earlier. Now that the temperature had fallen, she felt exposed to the elements as the wind slyly slipped under her outfit.

"I'm never far away," Lee Mile affirmed when they finally reached her vehicle. It was the best he could offer at that moment.

"I know," Marley said, smiling back into his shadowed face. He leaned into her, placing a kiss on her bare right shoulder. Within minutes, she was gone.

7

MS. ASHBY'S SHOP

He was always much stronger than she was. She never suffered because of it, though. His heart wouldn't let her. It was too big for anything less than the peace and love they shared. He was the rock and she the river spilling over his jagged edges.

They had made a home in a stained purple heart, four-room house Judah's uncle had given to him after deciding not to move back home. The lady from Germany had married him after all, which resulted in his relocating halfway across the world. By his word, Judah's uncle turned the house over to him for keeps.

When they first moved in, the house was half-finished. Judah put some old-time shutters over the windows that he had lifted off of a derelict home, which no longer had an owner. They gave the house a dated look that carried a strange appeal.

Judah stained the entire house himself. Inside and out. At the front, he bordered the pathway with rocks collected from Joe's River. Soon afterward, he commissioned a Ras by the name of Jah-Light to paint a mystic scene across a portion of the interior of the guard wall. The mural showed a pair of Rasta youths riding across the I-ration on the back of a lion. That scene led to an image of His Imperial Majesty and Empress Menen standing firmly next to The Church of Our Lady Mary of Zion, adorned with a rainbow arcing over it. At the end of the mural, a field of herb trees and a Rastaman beating a drum while his woman and children looked on, closed off the scene.

Judah was a man who found his meditation at its highest in his garden. The first evening Nubya went outside to help out, Judah did that thing he was known for doing whenever he disapproved of something. The silent conflict he would instigate weighed more than any amount of words that could be said. It wasn't always easy dealing with Judah. So, to keep the peace, Nubya made the house her jurisdiction by placing plants in every auspicious space offered up by each room.

Some days, Nubya would quietly observe Judah in his meditation as he planted up the garden beds or pruned the hedge. While he worked to beautify the grounds, she would sit out on the veranda steps, reading or picking at her toes— whatever tickled her fancy. It was these miscellaneous moments, amidst the clanking of the hoe into the dry earth, accompanied by reggae melodies seeping from the sound system speaker inside of their house, that she would sit in silence and enjoy Judah's quiet companionship.

From the front yard, they had a full view of the east coast and its bays. The lay of the land held the neighbors at a distance. But tamed vegetation at the front and sides of the house made the home inviting. The backyard was fenced in by a paling. Inside, some notable jewels, like the bamboo-enclosed outdoor shower Judah had styled in a fashion, similar to one he had seen at a west coast villa where he had done some construction work.

On the other side of the yard was a cabana with a mosaic tile floor. It housed a cooking and dining area, furnished by some mahogany chairs and a mismatched table that Judah had taken out of a skip at a house, which was being refurbished. The owners had no interest in the pieces, which they called, "old furniture." So Judah packed up his truck and carted them off to an antique shop. The shop's owner bought the best of the lot. The rest, Judah brought home.

This was their life for the past three years. Quiet. When they met, he was living in the north of the island with a brethren. She was sharing a government unit with her aunt and sister on the outskirts of town. To tell the truth, how they met was one of those things that just happened. One day, there was no Judah. The next day, there he was. In their courtship, they ended up making life on the windward side of the island, a good distance from both of their origins.

"Come ins" or "come yuhs" the neighbors would refer to Nubya, as most folks in the east came from the east. Everyone else, from wherever else, was grouped as foreign, except for people from other Caribbean territories. They were categorized as either Lucian, G.T., Trini, Jamaican, or, in Judah's case, Vincy.

Nubya was a seamstress turned fashion designer. Her small, successful clothing line led to a part-time instructor stint at the island's lone Polytechnic, where she taught dressmaking. Good fortune had made it possible that she could operate her clothing business from home, even hiring a sales and marketing associate, as well as an assistant tailor.

Nubya's clientele was faithful. They came from all over the island just to shop her designer line or to have custom outfits made by her. After winding through country roads to reach Nubya's atelier, clients then had to tackle the breath-snatching climb up the steep stairs that led to the front gate of her house. Some of the ladies griped about the trek, but it was Judah's silent quarreling that drove Nubya crazy even more.

To begin with, he didn't like the idea of how successful she had become, given the nature of the other work that took place at their home. Wary of having too many people around, it peeved him every time someone came calling because they had an appointment. At times, some clients proved excessively nosy. Others liked to count for the couple, factoring the home's decor and surroundings as they speculated about the occupants' prosperity, or lack thereof.

Some clients were presumptuous and liked to wander past the limits of the designated customer space, querying about the backyard or the garden, even going so far sometimes as to want a tour of the property. Judah preferred if the visitors kept their distance, but he would never dream of getting between Nubya and her work.

One plus one equaled two. Having more was always better than having less. If only he could redirect how Nubya's profession intersected with his lifestyle. So he rented the house at the bottom of the climb.

One day, just like that, Ms. Ashby finally died after being in this world for close to a century. She was a shopkeeper for all of her life and one who kept her financial success tucked away out of sight. Ms. Ashby was never extravagant or flashy. But when it came to her small abode with the shop affixed to the side, she never skimped on the upkeep of her property. For a house from its generation, its state was immaculate. It was so old that some claimed Ms. Ashby was even born there.

Ms. Ashby had never retired either, it seemed. After her death, her house remained closed up, which felt strange because so much life used to happen there. People were drawn to her and she to them. So she did what she loved for the people she loved—until the morning she decided she'd prefer her grave instead.

One afternoon, walking down to the main road, Judah spotted a real estate agent closing up the house after a viewing by some prospective tenants. A short conversation later, Judah convinced the agent to rent the house to him instead.

When Nubya got home that evening, she found Judah sitting, waiting for her on the front steps of Ms. Ashby's former home.

"I feel you should work from here," he greeted her as she came closer. She was puzzled to see him sitting there. "I will take care of the rent. You can cover everything else. There ain't no more reason for none of your customers to come up by us anymore."

8

DAUGHTERS

At night, the only way to navigate the steps that led to Nubya's abode was by flashlight. Unless the moon was out, there was no other way to cut a path through the pitch darkness, but by flashlight or memory.

"Bella Bella!" Marley's voice made its approach before she did.

Nubya was perched on the veranda, burning a fat spliff. "My woman, you can't tell time?" Nubya answered Marley's greeting in a loving, accusatory tone. Dressed in her favorite marigold-colored baby tee, the bottom of which she knotted at the base of her back, Nubya unwrapped her feet and stood up to reveal an army green camouflage batik wrap skirt, which flowed past her narrow ankles to brush against the ground.

"Oh, Lord! Muh girl! These stairs, though!" Marley replied, buying time with her lamentation. Making her way toward Nubya, Marley took a deep breath before launching into an explanation.

"I am so sorry I took so long. I stopped by the cemetery to put some flowers on my grandparents' graves. Guess who I ran into?" she asked as she gripped her body close to protect it from the cold of the night.

"Hmmmmm, sis!" Nubya embraced Marley with a huge hug, followed by a squeeze when she had finally reached arms' length. "Lee Mile," Nubya replied as they let go of each other.

"How did you know that?"

"How could I not know. I can see his energy all over you," Nubya said, smiling.

"I'm so sorry. He was having a get-together. Invited me over …"

"You couldn't say no … " Nubya mocked.

"I couldn't say no," Marley pouted, "and my phone had no service. I don't know what it is with out there by him. You can never get any service. Bet you it's some Obeah thing he's got going on," she instigated as she rubbed the sides of her upper arms, partially giggling at the absurdity of her claim.

"Bet you it's just Digicel's subpar service," Nubya shot back.

"But I have a Flow phone!" Marley corrected her. The irony of the situation made the two friends laugh.

"Do you have a shawl I can borrow? I forgot how cold it can get up here."

"Yeah, sis. Come," Nubya said as she invited Marley inside.

"Is he here?" Marley stage-whispered, slipping her sandals off at the door.

"No," replied Nubya in a normal speaking tone. "And why are you whispering?"

"You know how he is. All antisocial and stuff."

"He's not antisocial; he's private," Nubya protested, adjusting the distribution of her hair underneath her crocheted tam. They laughed again.

Nubya and Judah's home was cozy. The scent of incense was constant in their space. Incense sticks, wood incense, cones, oils, and fragrant candles. It didn't matter. Nubya burned them all. Entering the front house, a large Ites, gold and green Conquering Lion of Judah flag hung from the longest wall in the room. Under it, a small shrine stood.

A living room suite of mahogany Morris chairs was adorned by an abundance of mud cloth and earth tone hand-painted throw pillows. A large purple hammock that claimed a sizable chunk of the living room for itself gave the whole layout a rustic retreat vibe. Over in one corner stood a collection of Nyabinghi drums in assorted sizes; a waist-high bookshelf stood in another.

In the center of the living area, a flat handwoven basket, laden with fashion magazines, sat on top of a generous circular rattan rug, surrounded by three large floor cushions. The design of the cushion covers was Nubya's handy work, as were the surrounding sheer burnt orange curtains accented with tiny bells sewn onto the bottom corners of each panel.

Each time Nubya surveyed her home's interior, she marveled at her design touch. The thought of launching a rustic lifestyle-inspired home design line was tempting.

"Anyway, don't mind Judah. You know that you're good. So I don't know what you are play-worried about," Nubya assured. "I-Am messaged. Said she's going to pass by shortly."

"Is she bringing food, or did you cook?" Marley asked.

"Nah. I'm on my menses, so you know I can't touch a pot for Judah to see when it's that time of the month. I-Am said she will bring some of whatever is left back from the shop. Veg lasagna and some kind of salad. Not sure."

Marley held up her hand to reveal a shopping bag containing two bottles of natural wine. "I've brought drinks, but I'm not drinking. Had like two glasses too many of some palm wine Lee Mile's friend brought back from Senegal. It tastes good, but it's a bit too strong for my liking."

"You want something to burn, or you want to help me finish this?" Nubya extended her hospitality to include the partially smoked spliff she was nursing. Even though they could easily burn separately, there was a bond that came with sharing a ganja draw, which they still entertained.

"Is there fanta in it?" queried Marley. She could never understand why so many people added fanta to their herb. It was a next-day guaranteed visit to the toilet if she consumed it, which made it a no-no for her.

"Nah," Nubya assured.

"I need to eat first, though, before I end up knocked out on the floor," Marley assessed.

"Come! Let me roast you some corn."

"Yay!" Marley responded excitedly. "See why I can't help but make the trek all the way up here? Because I get goodies like roast corn!"

"I can't with you, though," Nubya responded, shaking her head in pretend disbelief. "To hear you talk, you would think that your stove doesn't work."

"You mean more like I don't *work* my stove," Marley confirmed.

They laughed themselves into the kitchen. Marley took a seat at the wrought iron table that rested up against the kitchen wall, surrounded by three chairs. Nubya began to gingerly roast two corn on the cobs over the open flame on the stove. When the kernels were charred to perfection, she returned them to their husks and rested the plate they were on between the two of them.

"So how is Lee Mile?" Nubya asked curiously between bites.

"He still looks good." Marley melted.

"I didn't ask how he looked. I asked how he was doing," Nubya chastised.

"He's good. He looks good. Smells good. He's good."

"Did you guys talk?"

"A little, but nothing in depth. There were a lot of people at the house. Then, this guy, the Senegalese guy who owns the restaurant in my building, turned up. They seem to be like besties or something. So it was all over from there," Marley concluded. With a second thought, Marley pondered, "Now, him? Yeah!" Marley smiled as she left the thought alone.

"Yeah, what?" Nubya pried.

"Yeah, and then some," replied Marley. They laughed out loud together again.

"You and your roving eyes. I'm good with my Kingstown lion," Nubya admitted, taking a sip of jamoon wine.

"Hear you! That man is too intense," Marley remarked, as she sat flipping the lid of Nubya's Zippo lighter with her right thumb. It was a gift from Judah to mark their first successful landing of Vincy herb as a couple.

"How you mean?"

"He just is," Marley reaffirmed.

"I like that, though," said Nubya, defensively playing with the bangles on her slender arms. "Unlike these clowns out here, he is on point. Like, I don't have to worry about a thing."

"Which is good. But couldn't he be on point and still be a bit chill?"

"I think it's sexy."

"Okay!" Marley gave up.

"Marley, all men, all people, have their ways. No one is perfect," Nubya reasoned, tucking her right foot under her left thigh.

"I'm not saying he has to be perfect. I just think he can cool out sometimes," Marley replied, searching Nubya's face.

"I like his intensity. I think it's hot."

"Okay. I'm not fighting you on this. He is a good man, but the fyah! Oh, Lawd! He does bring the fyah!" The inside joke made them chuckle again. There was always laughter whenever they got together. The concoction made for a strong bond—long conversations, plenty of reasoning, all wrapped up in love.

"What time is it?" asked Marley.

"Late."

"I-Am needs to hurry up."

"Look who's talking. Don't forget how late you were getting here," Nubya rebuked.

"I'm never late. I'm always on time, and my time is the right time." Marley exhaled a stream of smoke, aiming it at the rafters in the ceiling, then punctuated the thought with a smile.

"I wish you had come to my get-together the other night."

"Judah was out. The Shark was circling. I just wasn't in that mood. How was it? What did I miss?" Nubya asked, tapping the ash on the side of the glass ashtray now that the spliff was back in her possession.

"It was lit. I-Am came through with Shotta Forward. She's on this lollipop heights now."

"What! Are they good?" Nubya started to get excited. I-Am's alchemy was enchanting.

"Yeah. I think they can potentially be a hit. Especially for people who want to rec-create publicly without penalty."

"Yeah?"

"Yeah."

"If we get that going—the lollipops, baked goods, tinctures, all together—establish an optimal production output for return on investment, and lock off the market, we would be on to something really special." As she spoke, the fullness of the idea flashed right before Marley's mind's eye.

In tandem, the mathematics of the deal occupied Nubya's gray matter. "A lot of my clients burn, but I never sell to them like that. I keep it separate from my clothing business. But you see the lollipops, that would be different, especially if we focus on women. I find that men don't really like to see women burning herb. A lot of women prefer to be cute and stylish with it. We could create a whole line of recreational goods aimed at women. Eventually, we could even do a wine. That should be something I-Am could make. They make ganja wine in St. Vincent, you know?"

"Yeah?" Marley said, considering it.

"Yeah. They sell them like right in the market, like it's nothing," Nubya confirmed.

"Okay."

"But you know we would do it a certain how, with the packaging, etcetera. Nice it up. Brand it up. Marley, these things would sell," Nubya reasoned.

"The thing is, we have to be in a position, so when everything is said and done, we can come out of the shadows, ready for above-board operations. I don't mind the authorities hemming and hawing, play-acting like they don't know that decriminalization and legalization is the forward direction they must take. Their blasé attitude is a red herring to mislead so they can get their interests in place, while thwarting the viability of existing growers and smugglers. They want to be the ones who run things when the time comes to jostle for position as soon as that frontier opens up," Marley remarked.

There was a pause as the two pondered their venture.

"Are you going to tell Judah?" Marley finally asked, picking back up the conversation.

"I haven't decided yet. He doesn't need to know everything. We've been at this for a while, and I haven't said anything to him yet. Plus, too, sometimes my thing and his thing are different things. So I don't even think it is necessary," Nubya weighed out loud. "I don't know," she added irritably. "What I do know is that I just wish he would keep from around de Jamaican man."

"He's still here?" Marley asked, surprised.

"You know he can spend months at a time when he's ready. He claims it's 'cause the men keep paying him in local currency. So he has to convert that into U.S. currency, and that is what makes his stay take so long. Sometimes, I just want him gone so badly that I does be tempted to offer to convert the money myself, just so he would leave. But I does just stay humble," Nubya vented.

"That doesn't even make sense when you factor in the costs for him to linger about here," Marley countered.

"And all the money he spends on a guest house, etcetera," Nubya added.

"Plus, too, how is it that he, or even the men, are finding it so hard to find U.S. currency? That doesn't add up to me." Marley marveled at the situation, remaining unconvinced.

"Well, it's the excuse he gives in order to linger. I don't get in it, nor do I trust him."

"He knows about the runnings?" Marley asked.

"No. I don't think Judah would say anything 'cause it's none of that man's business. Furthermore, I wish Judah would shift he and just stick to maintaining his stash and to landing Vincy. But Bajans like Jam. Don't get me wrong. They like Bajan Green, as well. Probably more than Vincy. But you know Judah grows that hybrid strain and charges top dollar, so he needs the Vincy and Jam for his customers who come in at other price points. Me, I would just stick to one or two streams of income, and be done with that," Nubya protested, satisfied she had given sufficient thought to the situation to warrant her conclusion.

"Yeah, but he's trying to have as many lucrative revenue streams as possible because, if a shot gets lick up, and he has all his eggs in that one basket, it is hard to recover from that. You've been through that scenario already. You know it's not fun. Last time, it took months for y'all to catch back your hand properly," Marley reminded Nubya.

"It's true," Nubya admitted.

"You just want him to shake this Jamaican man. That's all."

"Exactly! I don't know why Judah needs to friends him at all!" Nubya exclaimed at the same time her phone vibrated on the table's top.

"I-Am?" Marley asked.

"Yeah. Coming back."

Nubya got up to go to the front gate to meet I-Am. Marley checked her social media accounts while she waited for the two to return.

"Sis!" I-Am exclaimed as she entered the kitchen a few minutes later, breaking the conversation she had started with Nubya on the outside.

"Ahhhh! Love and light, my dear," Marley reflected back. She reached down and placed her hands on the elastic waist of I-Am's royal blue harem pants.

"Your mommy always has you out late," Marley baby-talked to the protruding belly. "You were by me just the other night. Now you are here by Auntie Nubya's, out late another night. Don't worry. I know it is not your fault. You see, when you are born, and your mommy wants you to sleep at night so she can get things done, you will already be a night owl. She'll regret it then," Marley smartly declared.

"You are so wrong. That's not even funny. See the kind of things your friends does wish on you?" I-Am retorted, taking her customary draw from her Vicks inhaler.

"You smell good," Marley noted with a smile.

"I know." I-Am smiled back. "It's a Nigella oil ... vanilla something I'm working pun," I-Am teased.

"I'm starving," Nubya interrupted.

"I brought food," I-Am declared.

The three friends sat at the kitchen table, eating and talking. Talking and plotting. Plotting and planning. The way enterprising women with boss ideas talk at kitchen tables in the middle of the night.

Beautiful in contrasting ways, the three friends chatted until the sound of Judah's two-stroke scrambler, bearing down through the village road, cued Marley and I-Am that it was time to make their exit.

"Breakfast tomorrow by me," Marley suggested. "Bring Shotta, Zaire, and the youts. Around nine? Nubya ..."

Before Marley could finish, Nubya interjected. "Judah and I will be there. He has his ways, but you know he will come once you invite him."

Marley and I-Am exchanged looks.

"I'll return your Pyrex dish in the morning, I-Am," Nubya assured as she delayed cleaning up the kitchen so they could say their goodbyes. Hugs and kisses later on the veranda, Nubya watched her friends head out into the dewy night at the very moment Judah reached the front gate.

"Daughters. His Majesty Liveth," Judah respectfully greeted them, nodding his head reverently.

"Hail de I," Marley and I-Am chimed, mirroring him as they made their way past him, smiling sweetly in the dark.

"Guidance," Judah responded.

"Give thanks," I-Am called back as the two filed down the steps.

"See you tomorrow," Marley called out.

9

GULLY CREEPERS

Judah awoke at first light the next morning. The star-encrusted blanket of night still cloaked the sky when he buried his morning stiffness into an old pair of jeans, then sank his feet into a worn-out pair of steel-toed boots.

He slid on a vest. The threat of daybreak loomed over his stealth movements to get dressed. Judah eased out of the house, matched his stride to the wind, cleaving to the shadows as he wafted past village homes still asleep to become a ghost to the approaching day.

At the edge of his village, Judah cut through a narrow track that ran along the side of a field until it ended at the top of a nearby gully, where he began his descent. Waiting at the bottom of the gully's floor was Konjah Man, crouched down and enveloped by the predawn darkness that was intensified by the dense flora. Instinctively, Judah made his way over to his brethren, nodding his head to signal, a retreat further into the shaded area, a little way off from their usual meeting spot.

"Yeah, breddah, His Majesty Liveth." Judah spoke the greeting softly as Konjah Man rose to meet him.

"Hail de I. Rastafari. I and I. His Majesty Liveth," Konjah Man replied as they shook hands then leaned with bowed heads toward each other, as if in prayer. Anything of importance was always said in this stance. Nowhere else, and with no one else.

"Stinga confirmed that the Vincy men made it back safe." Judah lifted his head, continuing to speak softly yet firmly in the direction of Konjah Man's right ear. Not since they had stashed the Vincy men from Wednesday night's landing had Konjah Man and Judah spoken. Instead, they focused on executing all of the steps from their planned course of action that led to this morning's meeting.

From a young age, Konjah Man had a soldier-type personality. Once things were put in place, he seldom deviated from the script. His loyalty was refreshing, as was his dependability. Konjah Man wasn't that way because of mastery of self alone, but because he was a simple man, who cared not to veer away from instructions.

As a teenager in school, his relationship with pen and paper manifested as a contentious one, which caused his teachers to mistake his inability to relate to books as an inability to learn. Quite the opposite, Konjah Man was sharp. He understood the spoken word with more clarity than any instructions printed in black and white, taking what was said to heart once it passed his meticulous scrutiny for flaws and inconsistencies.

Judah had gone out with the Jamaican man and a few ones that Wednesday evening, and on his rounds, heard talk of a landing. Luckily, he was still in the environs of his home parish when the Regional Security System (RSS) aircraft, the Shark, made its appearance in the sky, quickly confirming the rumors.

Inwardly, Judah became alert. Itching to ditch the Jamaican man, he called home and checked in on Nubya. Afterward, he informed the Jamaican man that he was leaving to attend to wifey. Within an hour, he was in the company of Konjah Man, who had been keeping tabs on the boat's whereabouts—even stopping in at Judah's home to scope out the bays from the vantage point that the residence held.

Konjah Man knew every gully, track, bay, and spring that ran along coastal St. John. Judah understood the sea. Collectively, they had figured out the general vicinity in which the landing would have had to occur. They slid down to the secluded beach in time to butt up on two of the Vincy men from the night's landing, coming to shore with bales in tow.

The boat had begun to experience problems. The Shark was out circling the coy night sky, certain of illegal activity down below. The boat's captain bravely took a chance on the high tide and brought his vessel as close as he could into a nearby bay, dropping two of his men and their cargo overboard before retreating to the open waters, in hopes of playing possum until the coast was clear.

As luck would have it, the right beach for Judah was the wrong beach for the smugglers. The sight of the strangers immediately put the Vincy men on guard. But when Judah identified himself as a brethren willing to help his stranded fellow countrymen, things got resolved.

The four men organized quickly. Konjah Man and one

of the Vincy men cut through the strong, choppy Atlantic waters, swiftly swimming the remaining bales to shore. Judah and the other man cleared the cargo from the beach before the gangsters or Johnny Law reached the scene.

Konjah Man stashed the foreigners for the night in an opening on the hillside. He left them with only his and Judah's word of a twenty-four-hour return, complete with direct delivery to their boss to sustain them. Within that window of time, Judah sorted the cargo, taxed the best bales, and made sure the remainder reached its intended destination at the same time as the Vincy men.

Judah and Konjah Man lay low for a couple of days following. During that time, Judah busied himself parceling out and stashing their portion, while Konjah Man gathered intelligence from the streets.

"De men saying that you in power," Konjah Man said, uneasily relaying his findings, somewhat fazed by the talk he had heard.

"De men will wait," Judah responded, knowing that such talk was a prelude to purchasing inquiries when spoken by honorable men and a catalyst for robbery when coming from others.

"Everybody thinks that the shot get lick up and you is who steal Stinga herb. The police were out up to yesterday, still looking for de Vincy men. But Stinga got his men and the herb back. I made sure of that myself," Konjah Man reassured.

Loose talk had a way of getting Judah's head hot. A feeling of irritability that always arose whenever people gave their mouths too much freedom crept over him.

"I tired of these men coming up here, bringing

unnecessary heat 'round de place," Judah reasoned with restrained passion.

"We can't go into town, walk into these men neighborhoods, and start conducting business. So why they feel that they can come and land herb pun our beaches just so? Like it ain't nothing. Like they ain't got to reason wid nobody? Just come and go as they please. That fail!" Judah's face tensed with the release of each sentiment.

Judah's lean frame packed a lot of power. Ask the men from his past who he had chopped or slapped with his machete. They could attest to the might of his fury. If not for Nubya, that rage may have still been the currency of resolution for disagreements. It's not like she tried to change him, either. Domesticated men didn't appeal to her. It was more like he chose to humble to her sweetness.

"If it ain't one man risking, it's another. These men need teaching a lesson to understand that there is an order," Judah vented.

"We watching out for the Vincy men was an act of good faith. I could easily have given them to Babylon. But I don't want that kind of attention up here, and I don't ramp with the system like that. You see how Johnny Law does just make certain men lives miserable just because they know that these men does do things? Straight naggathon. Won't leave de men alone. You don't see police up here like that, stressing we. And I ain't trying to end up on their radar like that neither. Don't want the attention. Don't want the Defense Force trampling all about de place more than they already do. But when these men come up here, trying to call a shot, all them does do is bring unwanted attention," Judah reasoned.

"I ain't steal nothing. You see that kind of dangerous talk?" Judah weighed its street value. "I don't steal. De men need taxing so they can understand that there is a price for doing business up here. Plain and simple," he continued.

"De rest of men up here too soft. Too frightened when it comes to enforcing order," Konjah Man interjected.

"Yuh done know breddah!" Judah quickly agreed. "I tax the herb. I ain't steal nothing I-yah. They land a shot in my yard. My people save their people, protect them from Babylon, return de herb and all ... and they feel that it is what, a joke thing? Nah man!" Judah reflected.

"But you know these men goin' tell Stinga how much bales they haul up," Konjah Man speculated.

"I know. But I know Stinga knows how much bales he could have lost, too. Just because the boundaries ain't painted in the middle of de road don't mean a man can't tell when he has entered a new parish. Up here is St. John I-yah! They know they not home. Tread lightly and know that tax got to be paid. Simple."

"I will set the story straight when I make my rounds," Konjah Man offered. "Thinking to link Conqueror for some damage control. You know he is a boss at putting the right thoughts in people's heads."

"Yeah, man. I will talk to Shotta Forward, too. Have him set the story straight on his ends, in his realm. Can't let men wander the streets with the wrong idea yuh sight," Judah calculated.

Herb had a way of selling itself just off the strength of a mention. No one cared how you got it. The fact that you had it was enough. But Judah was an upright man. For him, how he got it was as important as him having it.

Unlike other men who would show off immediately as soon as they landed a shot or reaped a harvest, Judah was consistently patient and lowkey about his runnings. He always moved calmly in his endeavors, no matter how high the temperature of his feelings. It was how he had chosen to order his life.

Judah was never hasty when coming to market, either. The usual fears that other men entertained about being robbed or product going old, he seldom gave energy to. With calm, he would execute his strategy—certain in his formula, the loyalty of his soldiers, and main brethren.

"It's time to clean de Baje. Link with Zaire and pass by me around eight," Judah commanded Konjah Man, who nodded back in affirmation.

The Bajan Green had dried down and was ready for market. Konjah Man and Zaire were masters at cleaning buds, especially after I-Am had taught them that seeds were the true power and should be harvested, not sold willy-nilly.

Every time they sold a bud with a seed, they lost a chance at propagation. In turn, they strengthened the buyer's position to do just that, if he chose. If men wanted seeds, let them buy them separately, although close brethren would receive, if they asked. The absence of seeds essentially impacted the weight of a sale. Smart buyers understood they were getting more herb for their dollar with Judah's seedless bud. His unique value proposition never went unrewarded. Herb never got stale with Judah because it was never in his possession long enough to do so.

"You secure?" Konjah Man queried, concerned that with all the weight Judah now had around, men might risk coming at him.

"I safe," Judah assured, seeming to be simmering down.

"Some men already put in orders. So let me know what is what pricewise." Konjah Man delivered the heads up, having gathered the intel during his food rounds to different neighborhood blocks.

"Safe. What you dealing with, breddah?" Judah queried, intent on setting his brethren straight before anyone else.

"De usual. I good with that," Konjah Man confirmed.

Konjah Man had a different clientele from Judah. He catered to the men who would buy a draw or a ten bag, and on a good day, a twenty piece. Those types of transactions annoyed Judah. He never sold quantities smaller than eighths of an ounce, which eliminated the annoyances associated with having a large customer base of people continuously making small purchases.

Seeing a man every day on the block gave way to familiarity. Seeing a man bi-weekly kept the relationship in balance.

Judah ran his operation on exclusivity and integrity, even when he had to tax the occasional landing. He viewed it as justified. If his herb wasn't as hard as customers had come to expect, he would state that upfront. Men respected that and they were seldom disappointed. But what really made him choice was his tendency to add a smoke to a sale or let the weight go over just a bit.

In an environment where men moved hard mouthed with their product, Judah's generosity was a distinguisher. So he never had to rush to hustle because, in his view, herb wasn't a hustle. It was a holy sacrament, which he tried to protect from the capitalist mentality the streets had brought to the game.

Not wanting to leave Nubya alone for too long, Judah wrapped up the reasoning with Konjah Man. In tandem, they stepped back from each other. Parting ways, they headed in opposite directions to how they had arrived at their meeting on the gully's floor.

PART II

10

JUDAH'S STORY

On Judah's first visit to Barbados, he washed up on the coarse sands of Stroud Bay, St. Lucy. That night, when the shots fired, Judah took an agentive leap into the chilly, shark-infested waters off the northwest coast of the island.

Half a day earlier, he had boarded a twin-engine pirogue, leaving Chateaubelair for the treacherous haul to Barbados —with instructions in his head, a push-button cell phone secured in a waterproof case, and the clothes on his back.

Judah suited up in courage as the boat glided out from the embrace of the quiet fishing village to greet the seemingly infinite quality of the open water. The evening was thick with expectation. Cutting across the voluminous sea, a young Judah watched as his mountainous island home melted away into the horizon, and the horizon into the encroaching nightfall.

It was his first run. The boat sprinted like a hurdler across the wild waters for several hours. But that didn't stop Judah from wolfing down the starchy meal his uncle shared with him from his flask. Judah's constitution was strong. Instead of being sickened by the ride, if anything, the boat's incessant battle with the sea swells made Judah hungrier than he had ever been.

Smuggling was a job that required patience, amongst other virtues. The monotony of the journey, coupled with the newness of the experience, wore on Judah's nerves. He had already identified all of the heavenly bodies, recited his uncle's instruction to himself numerous times, entertained lost thoughts, and conjured up dreams for his future. Knowing that Barbados was a mere ninety miles away supported the idea that it was just within reach; but the reality of the open water trek spoke otherwise. Eventually, Judah grew weary of staring into nothingness and fell into an unsettled sleep.

A Vincentian by birth, Judah's uncle grew up primarily in Barbados with his father's family in the parish of St. John. However, his ties to his Vincy homeland were held firm by both of his parents. His father was a fisherman, who used his boat to transport fruits and vegetables from St. Vincent to Barbados for his Vincentian wife, who was a hawker, to sell in Bridgetown's Cheapside market.

For Judah's uncle, growing up in this life was also his school. His parents speculated goods between the islands until old age interceded, passing those roles onto the three children who showed genuine interest.

In the end, when life eventually slowed down, Judah's uncle's father took root in Barbados, while his mother lived out the remainder of her days in St. Vincent. Like his father, Judah's uncle was a seaman. Unlike his father, his primary cargo was fish and ganja.

Judah's mother, Mary, could no longer handle him. They had been close before. But when his father went lost at sea in the latter part of Judah's teenage years, the anger that was awakened by the unsolved mystery sparked a rage that scared his mother and everyone around him. So she pleaded with his uncle, her brother-in-law, to help her find a solution.

Perhaps sailing the open waters would quell his demons. Maybe the quest of continuing to look for his father would soothe his pain. Behind the fury, Judah's uncle saw a hurting young man. That hurt Judah's uncle in return. So he made it a point of inviting Judah along with him on fishing expeditions, hoping that time spent in the ocean's presence would purge Judah of his affliction. Maybe he wouldn't be so mad all the time. Perchance, he could even forgive the sea for what she had done and someday love her again.

Samuel tapped Judah's shoulder to rouse him. He was Judah's uncle's closest friend, an expert seafarer and the third man on the job. In the distance, dots of golden flecks of light floated above the horizon like a necklace worn by some indigo being. Judah pushed his sleepiness away and allowed the excitement of the prospect of their mission to fill him. Fear crept in, but he quickly replaced it with alertness.

The beauty of the limestone isle, softly lit on the opaque waters at an intersection where the Atlantic Ocean meets the Caribbean Sea, was sublime. But Barbados' waters were tricky waters, swarming with obstacles. Judah had heard stories of Stroud Bay, Archer's Bay, Maycocks Bay—the holy trinity of drug holes, as the local men would refer to them.

Judah's uncle had warned him about Bajan men, as well. Whereas Vincy men were farmers, looking to make an honest living in the ganja trade after the WTO decimated

St. Vincent's banana industry via free trade agreements, Bajan men were gangsta hopefuls, seduced by the lure of the drug trade the movie industry had mesmerized them with.

More accurately, they were wannabe badmen from a pacifist stock of forefathers who were proud of being given their freedom, having never had the courage to pursue it in any meaningful way. Judah was coming from the land of Joseph Chatoyer and Spirit Cottle to the home of Bussa and Winston Hall.

The wind whipped up a greeting that demanded Samuel maneuver the boat expertly as they sized up to the flashing signal sprinting out from the darkness to indicate their landing point ahead. Judah took a deep breath for a quick last-minute gear-up to prepare mentally. On his exhale, Judah's mind wandered for all but a split second.

Gunshots fired!

In one springing motion, Judah's uncle leapt toward him and instinctively brought Judah crashing down to the floor of the boat. Samuel fired back as it soon became clear that the first shooters were not coast guards, but pirates coming to lick up their runnings. The probing spotlight, the amplified voice demanding surrender, all were missing. Samuel let some more shots fly into the darkness in the direction of the aggressors. Judah's uncle began dumping bales into the sea.

This was why men never liked to ship weight with a bunch of other men, especially ones they didn't know. Men were known to talk too much, tell their girlfriends everything, boast to other men, try to accommodate other men in the runnings to reduce costs—all things that left them exposed to sabotage. Catching a slight glimpse of the silhouette of the marauder vessel against the scant backlight from the island, Samuel fired off more rounds.

"Remember what I said. Hear?" Judah's uncle cautioned while he hastily lowered the last bales into the sea. "Stick to de plan, no matter what," he hurriedly reminded Judah, who was poised to make a soundless entry into the water.

Judah hesitated. He had never been to Barbados before. He wasn't bulletproof. He had no clue where he was going, even though he had been told what to do. For the first time in the two years since the fury had overtaken Judah, in that vulnerable moment, his uncle glimpsed the soft-hearted young man that once occupied that body. Life returned to Judah with the threat of death nearby.

Judah jumped ship. He gathered as much cargo as he could manage and headed in the direction of the last flicker of light he had seen before the ambush—mindful of his enemy floating about under the cloak of darkness. More shots exchanged, but Judah couldn't make out who was firing them.

He was a fierce swimmer, but the swells of water battled him. The sea had suddenly become rough, as if agitated by the crossfire. The strong currents knocked Judah about, threatening to pull him away from his shoreline trajectory. But his determination kept him on course.

There were things in these waters worse than bullets and sharks. Like being slapped upon the spikey colonies of razor-sharp black rocks that would dig chunks of flesh from the unfortunate swimmer's body, the prospect of which sounded less excruciating than the actual occurrence itself.

Thoroughly unkind to terrestrial intruders, black rocks couldn't be touched, held, nor walked upon without protection. These slabs of torture tightly guarded the sandy bays within their clutches, mercilessly ripping boats and men apart that the tides had flung upon their laps. Hidden within the crevices of the rocks, resided sea urchins, whose long spines that folks referred to as needles were known to cause men unmentionable pain.

Judah swam for his life. Inadvisably, he fought against the ocean currents. Struggled to keep his head immersed in the air. Light-headedness began to set in from the influx of water coursing through his nostrils, draining his sinuses of their last store of mucus.

When the sea threatened to take his cargo, he gripped it even tighter. When she dumped a wave over his head, pushing him to the ocean's floor, he kicked himself free to the surface again, determined that, unlike the netting of his father, she would not seize his life.

Judah struggled for what felt like an eternity. Valiant in his efforts. It was the confrontation he had in secret, longed for. *How dare she! How dare she!* he battled.

For the first time since he had lost his father. For the first time since the fury came. For the first time since that lifetime ago—Judah parted ways with all that ate at him slowly inside and released himself from his inner abyss. For the first time since the advent of his manhood, Judah wasn't angry with the sea and her mysterious ways. He just wanted to live.

The tide washed Judah's fatigued body onto the shore, leaving him exposed to the night. Though determined to continue on to reach the flicker of light he held in his memory, Judah's limp frame remained collapsed where it lay. Catspraddle, the sea had deposited him upon a layer of sargassum seaweed that reeked with a repulsive rawness. Its softness was a welcoming cushion for his weary body. Judah tried to raise his head, but it refused to move.

This is not the time to be weak, he inwardly told himself. *Move!* he commanded.

But nothing came of it. His cognitive self half-listened to the sounds of his surroundings, trying to make out his environment during the quiet that came with the retreat of the waves. The gunshots had stopped. He listened again. Footsteps were approaching.

Move! his mind commanded his body, to no avail.

"Come!" a rough voice suggested in a hushed tone. "Come!" it reached out again.

A strange hand gripped Judah's arm. The intentions of the stranger met with Judah's will at that moment, causing his weak body to come alive again.

Judah arose sluggishly. His limbs immediately slumped under the weight of being on terra firma. His eyes still burned from the saltiness of the seawater. Looking around at his immediate surroundings, he began to catch his bearings.

As his eyes adjusted to the absence of light, he spotted the outline of four bales scattered across the seaweed a short distance from the water's edge. In front of him, an unfamiliar soul that kept giving out instructions. Judah's mind went into questioning mode. Where was his uncle? Where was Samuel? Where were the gunmen in hot pursuit?

"You carry one and I carry one," the voice commanded.

"Nah, you carry two and I carry two," Judah reasoned back, catching himself.

Cutting across the sandy bay, they proceeded to hike the face of the gully, maneuvering through the blistery manchineel trees along a loose path that caused Judah to stumble several times. Upon reaching the top, the two men stashed away behind an embankment. Some feet away, the back of a village slumbering to their 'fore day morning activities. Scoping out the scene, they spotted the quick flicker of lights from the approaching vehicle that was quietly creeping through the track toward them.

"I need to reach Gideon," Judah finally admitted. "Do you know who that is?"

"Yes I," his partner in crime answered back. "Come."

11

THE UPPER ROOM

The vintage white Suzuki Carry van reversed into a galvanized steel garage affixed to the compound. A solitary streetlight on the front road abutting the premises exposed a bright yellow wall that gave way to a forest green painted pair of garage doors at the end of the lot, which stood guard once they had shut the vehicle and its occupants inside.

Four men of varying heights, dressed in all-black tracksuits and matching black tams upon their heads, filed out of the minivan quietly. They relegated an uncomfortably damp Judah to standing in their midst as they escorted him through the back entrance of the garage and onto the main compound.

Purposefully, they made their way across the yard to an elevated wooden structure that carried alertness, even during the ungodly hour of their approach. At its exterior, the men with the black tams halted. Collectively, they saluted the structure then dispersed, leaving Judah standing cold and clammy in the middle of the compound, feeling lost.

Judah looked around, trying to make sense out of his surroundings. He noticed the guard wall had a pedestrian entrance gate, but it appeared to be locked. Turning around, he surveyed the sparsely placed solar lights that illuminated the pathways to various structures.

At the side of the building where he stood, there was a collection of doors that reminded him of entrances to water closets. Next to that was a structure that resembled an office or some type of administrative building. Across from there, a canteen area, dominated by a repurposed shipping container, that entertained a couple of rows of lunch benches arranged herringbone-style in front of it.

In the distance, three women dressed in full-length cotton boubous descended the incline at the opposite end of the yard, coming from what Judah reasoned was some kind of living quarters. It was the same direction the black tam entourage had, minutes ago, disappeared to with the four bales from the beach.

The three women floated toward Judah, adorned with turban headwraps, which they balanced like crowns upon their heads. On their faces, they wore looks of deep concern. Arriving within conversation distance of a shivering Judah, they paused in the brightest spot of the dimly lit area and respectfully delivered their greeting.

"Hail, breddah. His Majesty Liveth." They welcomed the stranger with a semi-bow.

"Hail," Judah responded, vaguely familiar with the vocabulary of this language, having heard it spoken before by Rastas from his island home.

Judah had encountered Rastas before. Locs men, too. Locs men, with their salon-styled matted hair, could be found anywhere, doing just about anything. But Rastas, with their peculiar order and indignant livity, were devotees of the Ethiopian emperor, Haile Selassie I.

The prophet Marcus Mosiah Garvey had advised his people, the descendants of stolen Africans pirated to the Caribbean and the Americas by European traders, to look to the east for the coming of a great king. It was a clarion call to stoke the revival of negritude, as an encroaching demise of self upon the stolen people approached its fourth century of dominance.

On the second day of November, one thousand, nine hundred and thirty years after the Roman Christ walked the earth, Garvey's prophecy was made manifest. On that day, Ras Tafari Makonnen, the 225th descendant of the biblical King Solomon and the Queen of Sheba, ascended to the throne. Coronated as the Conquering Lion of the Tribe of Judah, His Imperial Majesty Haile Selassie I, King of Kings of Ethiopia, Elect of God.

In the West Indies, out of the womb of Jamaica, the spiritual children of Rastafari came forth and spread throughout the region, awakening the consciousness of other descendants of stolen ones across the Caribbean. Those who saw the light returned to a life as guardians of the earth. They embarked upon a livity of emancipation from mental slavery, builders of family, community healers, conscious guides, creators of beauty, definers of identity—followers of His Imperial Majesty.

The ancestral spirit of Uganda's Queen Nyabinghi arose and manifested through the music of the kettle drum, imprinting a heartbeat rhythm into the songs of rebellion and freedom that permeated souls across the world through Rasta music ... reggae music.

The revolutionary Mau Mau of Kenya, with their militant matted locs, influenced the Rastas' way of growing their hair. This look caused dread within the weak-hearted, drunken by the illusionary poison of sanctified oppression, which caused them to hunt early adherents of Rastafari. To survive, Rastas were forced to retreat deep into rural areas to escape being trimmed, jailed, or, in worst cases, killed by the civilized colonial forces.

King James's version of biblical accounts still held nuggets of truth. So Rastas harvested the wisdom in the words and used it to construct the foundation for the ideology of their order. Mother Nature brought forth the holy sacrament of ganja to elevate the conscious vibration of this emerging collective, amplifying Rastas' ability to ride the heavens in their pursuit of spiritual heights.

"Who does de I wish to see?" asked the Rastafari woman standing in front of Judah.

"Who am I talking to?"

"Yashimabet, first daughter of Zion, the one who is tasked to welcome de I," she responded. With her arms resting on the front of her thighs, she allowed the fingertips of both of her hands to meet in the form of an upside-down triangle that pointed toward the ground.

"I asked for Gideon. They tell me if things go wrong, and I end up in Barbados, to ask for Gideon. I ask the Ras at the beach if he knew Gideon, and he said yes and brought me here," Judah recounted.

"De I cold?" Yashimabet queried.

"Yes."

"Hungry?"

"Definitely."

"Tired?"

Judah nodded defeatedly.

"Accepting these things which I and I offer de I is an embracing of the way ones operate here, with full acknowledgment of de I respecting de order. Overs?"

"Overs," Judah resigned.

"The bathroom is that unit across there with the four doors," Yashimabet pointed out graciously. "The shower is around the back. The last two doors are rooms where de I can get ready. After, have a seat on that side." She signaled to the canteen area. "They will come for de I."

The two other women that were with Yashimabet came forward, one with a towel and toiletries, the other with clothes, slippers, and a biodegradable garbage bag for Judah's wet garments.

Judah finished bathing and dressing. At the canteen, he found himself in the company of a couple, up before first light, preparing breakfast for the residents of the compound. They offered Judah a hot bowl of oats porridge flavored with coconut milk and sweetened with molasses. Just as Judah lowered the spoon from his last mouthful, a tall, lanky brethren appeared and escorted him over to the residential side of the compound.

Judah was received in the Upper Room. A spiritual space. Seated on the floor, he scanned the circle of brethren in whose presence he sat. Unlike the brethren from earlier, each man's black tam was removed to reveal a bevy of locs. Clumped into various expressions of uniqueness and lengths, each man's crown complemented the personality of its owner.

Gideon sat distinguished within the group. His locs cascaded over his shoulder and down the front of his torso, draping across his forearm. The ends of his hair coiled in his lap like a cobra in a basket.

Gideon's sunken face was crossed with lines that aged him far beyond his years. His skin was like worn leather that held on dearly to the face that looked up to engage Judah in conversation. Scanning for broken parts, his full knowledgeable eyes peered deeply into young Judah.

Judah would learn that morning that the run from St. Vincent was Gideon's call. Gideon was an associate Judah's uncle had worked with over the years. They had been through enough scenarios together to suspect sabotage might have been in the mix when Samuel informed Judah's uncle of some hurried shot a town man called in. The rising kingpin pressed matters by cashing in on a previous favor Samuel had owed to legitimize the deal. The story went over young Judah's head. Fatigue prevented him from dissecting the details.

The reasoning amongst the men went on for a long time. At various points in the rising of the thick ganja smoke that levitated over the domes of those gathered in the room, Gideon assured Judah he had done well. By the time Judah passed out in the circle from fatigue, fowl cocks were already on full blast, crowing calls and responses across the yard that a new day had arrived at the compound of the Church of Haile Selassie.

HAILE SELASSIE IS THE CHAPEL

It was Quartus who noticed the cut that ripped through the muscle at the back of Judah's upper right arm. Judah passed out so hard during the reasoning that Gideon ordered two of the brethren to lift him to the guest quarters.

Unhooking his arms from around their necks in the process of laying him down upon the bed, Quartus touched the wound by accident. Pulling up Judah's sleeve, Quartus met face on with a nasty gash that would require stitches and care.

Judah slept for two days straight. The morning of the third day, he rose to the sound of chanting in the distance. He was vaguely familiar with Rasta speak, but this language was different—new to his ears.

Judah tried to get out of bed, but every muscle in his body was stiff and sore. He pressed down onto the mattress to propel his body upward, only to be confronted with a sharp pain that shot down his arm, flooring him.

Using his left hand to investigate the tender region from

which the pain originated, Judah discovered four inches of bandaged gauze, which he later found out was covering seven stitches.

Three other cots occupied the dormitory where he stayed. Judah walked past the beds, neatly made up with a soldier-like precision, and headed outside in pursuit of a toilet. There was not one in sight.

After emptying his full bladder by a hedge, Judah continued to follow the reverend sounding chants. He headed down the concrete slab stairs that led from the residences and ventured across the compound, where he found himself at the foot of the structure the men in black tams had saluted days earlier.

In the daylight, Judah beheld the fullness of the simple wooden structure, which was painted a cheery yellow. The windows were closed, as were the doors, but voices inside still managed to permeate the walls. In chorus, the occupants chanted the unusual refrains supported by what sounded like the continuous tinkering of tiny bells, a concoction that left him fully intrigued.

Judah, like a man possessed, approached the staircase. On his way up, he stumbled over a deposit of shoes piled outside the entrance. He had never felt anything like this pull that made him feel compelled to be present. But, for what, he did not know.

Judah waited at the doors with anticipation. Moments later, they finally reopened, as did the windows. A cloud of frankincense smoke escaping into the open air washed over him. He felt transported. Bravely, Judah proceeded to step inside of the structure.

It was a church, fashioned like other churches he had

seen before but punctuated with notable differences. The brethren at the entrance, wearing an Ites gold and green sash, halted Judah before he could go in any further.

"Greetings, breddah," he declared cheerfully. "You may enter once you have removed your shoes."

Without hesitation, Judah flipped his footwear to the side. But the brethren with the sash had more for Judah to do.

"Walk up the aisle to the altar and do this when you reach the top," he demonstrated.

"Huh?" a puzzled Judah responded. So the brethren reissued the instructions as best he could, while the church service continued on, oblivious to the intrusion of the guest.

"When you are coming back down the aisle, walk backwards and take a seat on that side with the men," the sash-wearing brethren continued as he handed Judah a small booklet of liturgy accompanied by a bible, for use later.

Judah awkwardly followed the instructions as best he could. He took a seat in a half-empty pew at the back of the church. Sitting there, Judah became aware of himself for the first time since he had urinated in the hedge earlier. He felt rested but sore. Curious but fulfilled. Welcomed.

Judah looked around at everything, but only his eyes moved. To his right sat modestly dressed women, orbited by a number of youths. On his side of the church, a mix of men sat attentively, some with their male youths by their side. The entrances of the church were guarded by the sashed men. At the altar, robed brethren circled what Judah would later learn was a symbolic replica of the Ark of the Covenant.

To say Judah was mesmerized would be to trivialize his

experience. He had seen brotherly love before. He knew of unity, but the order and authority that these brethren displayed reached directly into the new space Judah had cleared out that night in the sea, filling him with reverence.

The sermon was fiery. Judah had no clue what half of the ruckus was about. But the reasoning resonated with something inside of him, opening doors to consciousness that, until now, had remained locked.

From what Judah had gathered from the charismatic robed man with the single bongo loc that stuck straight up about half a foot into the air—the Twelve Tribes, Bobo Shanti, and Nyabinghi were all misinformed about Rastafari. In truth, the church held the truth and was the way, just as the crown prince had ordained it.

At the conclusion of the sermon, after the robed men had circled the replica Ark the ordained number of times, they lined up at the altar in preparation to descend into the body of the church. Instinctively, those congregation members seated at the windows reached out and closed all of them in. The sashed men at the doors closed those too.

Standing ceremoniously, the chanting began again, with everyone within earshot donating their voices as they recited the words with conviction. The robed brethren leading the procession controlled a gold-plated censer that he rhythmically rocked back and forth, filling the house of worship with smoke from the burning frankincense within.

The chanting intensified. Judah caught on that the end of each refrain concluded with, "Haile Selassie I." Row by row, the procession went about systematically blessing the members of the congregation as they made their way down the center aisle. The procession, led by the robed figure yielding smoke from the censer, who led another carrying a holy book high above his head, followed by another robed brethren holding an oversized ceremonial golden Axum Cross, eventually arrived at the final pew at the back of the church.

Judah was the last person in the congregation to receive a blessing. Prostrating in the manner he had seen displayed by members before him, a young Judah bowed his head and allowed the prayers of the robed brethren, carried on the smoke from the censer, to envelope him.

A robed Quartus then made his approach and hovered an oversized wooden six-point star engraved with scriptures above Judah's head and proclaimed, "The Lord loveth the gates of Zion more than all the dwellings of Jacob."

Confidently, Judah responded in the same manner he had heard professed by others around him and declared, "Glorious things are spoken of thee, O city of Jah. Selah. I will make mention of Rahab and Babylon to them that know me, behold Philistia, and Tyre, with Ethiopia; this man was born there. And of Zion it shall be said, 'This and that man was born in her and the highest himself shall establish her. The Lord shall count when he writeth up the people, that this man was born there. Selah.'"

13

A FI FLY OUT

Two weeks later, Judah's uncle visited the church's compound in the highlands of Boscobel, St. Peter. Since attending his first church service, Judah had made up his mind that this was where he wanted to be.

"I want to stay here," Judah reasoned to his uncle in a private conversation down by a spring that cascaded through a remote point, past the residential area of the compound.

Walking as they talked, their conversation led them into a partially tamed area of the I-ration, depositing them by a wallaba pole, turned seating, near the banks of the spring. In Barbados, it was said that every bush was a man. So cautiously, each spoke his piece, ever mindful of their surroundings.

"Your mother is asking for you. When I returned without you, she swear blind I gone and kill her only son. She near kill me when I tell her that I left you in Barbados," Judah's uncle explained.

Judah bowed his head. Running his fingers over his hair, he realized that it hadn't been cut since he left home. *The girls will probably freak out if they see me with my uncombed hair knotted up like this,* he thought.

"How mum?"

"She's good. Vex, but good. You know how women get in these types of situations. Well, that is how she is right now."

"Uncle, I don't know how to describe what I'm feeling, living up here with these bredren."

"You don't have to tell me. I know Gideon for a while now, even before he get deported and became a priest."

"What?"

"Don't tell him I tell you anything, eh. But he's that kind of chap. People are easily drawn to him."

"Why was he deported?"

"He would have to tell you that himself. Right now, my only concern is getting you back home."

"I'm not feeling that, though."

The conversation came to an impasse and petered out for a bit. Each man retreating to his inner thoughts.

"Well, if you going to stay here, there is a right and a wrong way to do it," Judah's uncle finally surrendered. "For your mother's sake, and so she don't end my life, I want you to do this the right way."

"And how is that?"

"Come with me back to SVG, and let me put you on a plane to Barbados. I can work on getting you some kind of status because, in the absence of your father, I is you father now. And you're still at the right age for me to claim you as mine."

"Uncle!" young Judah protested.

"Judah, work with me, nuh. Just work with me," his uncle pleaded.

The second time Judah came to Barbados, it was on a delayed LIAT flight that had the church brethren who had come to collect him waiting for hours at the airport for his arrival. When Judah finally emerged from the arrival hall, he was greeted by a smart smile, punctuated by a gold cap on the top right second incisor.

Quartus's rough voice that first greeted Judah on the beach months back, now greeted him at the airport. Gripping Judah's hand with effervescence, Quartus welcomed his brethren and declared, "His Majesty Liveth!" to which Judah echoed his sentiments in reply.

With one suitcase in tow, Judah boarded the vintage white Suzuki Carry van and began his new life as a reborn man in Barbados.

14

THE CONQUERING LION

For eight years, Judah dwelled in the highlands of Boscobel. A natural-born leader, he grew into an intelligent young man, molded by discipline and devotion to the scriptures.

Judah's life was a simple one. He lived on the compound in a dorm room, which he shared with three other brethren. A cot to sleep on and a chest of drawers for his belongings was the sum of his possessions.

Hailing from various West Indian islands, collectively, the church's members were devoted to a shared, common goal: working tirelessly to reinstate His Majesty's empire from their Caribbean outpost in Barbados. Through the church's various commercial and community initiatives, Judah was always busy. He selflessly donated energy and risk to the cause. An avid reader, in his free time, however, he studied all manner of topics, especially people.

Barbados easily became home. His work with the church constantly kept him on the road. Judah gradually learned about the island and its people on many of his trips to various districts in the course of conducting the church's business.

In the quaint northern city of Speightstown, the church had secured a property deal that allowed them to establish a vibrant retail niche. Within Judah's time at the church, they constructed a number of stalls, out of which they primarily sold items that members had made or grown themselves—leathercraft, clothes, art, jewelry, dried goods, preserves, fruits, vegetables, and Ital food. A portion of the stall spaces were rented out to interested persons outside of the church community. With the rent collected from those tenants, the church was able to cover the overall cost of doing business in the space.

Some called the Speightstown locale the "Temple Yard of the North," after the original Rastafari market space, Temple Yard, located in the southern capital, Bridgetown. For Judah, it was the campus of his university of life.

Although Judah enjoyed his work with the church, he slowly grew disenchanted with its leadership. He had submitted to the Most High and daily gave respect and service to the leaders who, in his view, deserved honor at all costs. Through them, the Most High had revealed himself, which made them sacred beings unto the Most High.

Judah had allowed the church to temper his temper with their liturgy, order, and doctrine. But there were things about their leader, Gideon, that at times, would cause Judah to simmer inwardly. Something which Judah concealed from the world.

Gideon spoke a good game. However, at crucial times, his reasonings were way off, his logic tilted, and his leadership was questionable. Like the time in a reasoning session when Judah asked quite innocently, "Which church does the current descendants of the monarchy attend for their weekly service? The historic Ethiopian Orthodox Church or the newly established Church of Haile Selassie?"

Infuriated by the insolence, Gideon chastised Judah for two hours non-stop. At no point did he answer Judah's question. Instead, he opted to dissect perceived flaws in Judah's character. The days that followed, Judah then found himself mysteriously isolated from his brethren, as if placed on social probation.

Another time, Judah queried as to which church would be the church of the monarchy once it was restored. Would they go with the church founded by Menelik, the son of Solomon and the Queen of Sheba, or would a new Ethiopia adopt the Church of Haile Selassie as the church of the state? For the three weeks that followed the question, Judah's workload increased two-fold. At every turn, Gideon found cause to admonish Judah in the presence of his brethren. Again, his question went unanswered.

The elders tried to proselytize Judah into baptism, in hopes that crossing into the faith would quell his invasive questioning and curiosity about things he should just accept. That didn't sit well with him either. To Judah's mind, he welcomed the framework the church had provided for ones to organize and centralize. He had also grown up hearing ones refer to Rastafari as a livity, not a religion. Something he had yet to reconcile within his heart.

And what about the other branches of Rastafari—the Nyabinghi, Twelve Tribes, Bobo Ashanti—along with ones who sighted His Majesty, even though they were not a member of any sect? Were they to be disregarded simply because they were not churchical?

Eventually, unable to resolve where he stood within his ideologies, Judah turned to his trusted brethren Quartus. If ever Judah had a soul brother who walked upon the earth, Quartus was he.

Quartus was a high-spirited brethren whose presence always elevated the surrounding vibe. He was also a straight talker. He could tell a man the worst things about himself and get that said man to agree with him jovially. Quartus had mastered the art of delivery, having figured out that *how* things were said always helped people digest *what* was being said.

Quartus held his own thoughts about the church, but his love for Selassie held strain. Quartus loved His Majesty so much that he gave into baptism, and like his other brethren, had received a new identity signified by a biblical name. His was Quartus.

Quartus, like Judah, had found purpose through the church. This caused him to bury his own frustrations behind his smile. One evening, as Quartus and Judah reasoned about life, Quartus shared the unfortunate story of the banishing of his fiancée from the church. Gideon's logic had tilted yet again. Without hesitation, he reasoned away Quartus's woman of several years from associating with or coming to the church. Quartus was torn.

There were discrepancies in Gideon's personality as well. The collected, distinguished gentleman Gideon showed to the world was often undermined by a stinking-attitude Gideon, which he would only show to his charges. Too many times, Gideon's pre-deportee personality would emerge from where it lurked. When it did, his gangsta priest persona would more than rub Judah the wrong way.

For eight years, Judah reassured himself that he was serving God, not the personality of the leadership. But as the years went on, it became increasingly hard to see God through the stain of personality.

Judah had a temper and though he had rid himself of the fury that had temporarily haunted him, it left him with a residual temper, which he struggled to master. With the passing of the years, he felt his temper gradually nearing the compound. Sometimes it longed to enter the Upper Room; other times, it waited, standing at the door of the church. Some days, it rolled up and did a drive-by in the streets. Mostly, Judah's temper would simmer wherever Gideon's lack of respect or offside reasoning reared its ugly head.

One day, late in year eight, Judah's temper finally showed up, ready to take the reins on a confrontation between him and Gideon. Unbeknownst to Gideon, he had summoned Judah's temper with one of his out-of-place comments and worsened the already bad situation by allowing his pre-deportee, street-hustler alter ego to roam the compound unrestrained for nearly a week!

Judah held council with his temper, explaining that he had worked hard to become the type of man he was. He didn't want to ruin it with an outburst. He reasoned that he could not allow his temper to ravage the compound because he respected the people who resided there and the bonds they had made. He disclosed that he had climbed too high to let someone's personality bring him low.

His temper countered that there was only so long that it could sit by and watch Judah be demeaned by Gideon's personality. There was a way that men treated men, and this was not it. No matter how passionate Judah felt about the cause. No matter how devoted he was to His Majesty. No matter how grateful Judah was for finding a place in this churchical family.

Sensing that his temper could only be restrained for so long, Judah resolved within himself that it was time to go. He had grown from a teenager to a man in this place. More so, he had become a valued and respected member of his community. He had fallen in love with the teachings of His Majesty, inherited a family of ones, who he had cared for dearly and had constructed himself into the upright man he desired to be. But the season for his time with the church was now over.

The day Judah released that thought into the universe with earnest, he met Nubya. The day after that, a long-awaited job opportunity at the solar power plant came through.

As a man, Judah reasoned with Gideon that he had outgrown living on the compound and was moving to the village of Clinketts, a few minutes ride away from his new job in the northern parish of St. Lucy. If he stayed at the church, it meant living in a two-fare zone and making a daily two-hour commute each way, a burden he had no desire to carry. It was a convenient truth.

By the end of the month, Judah unceremoniously left the compound. A few weeks later, Quartus admitted to Judah that he too, was leaving the church. Judah suggested that Quartus move in with him and rent the second bedroom of the chattel house he was living in.

A month after, Quartus moved in with Judah. A year

later, Quartus set aside his baptismal name and returned to the beloved name of his choosing: Konjah Man. He reunited with the banished mother of his prepubescent son and moved back to his hometown parish of St. John to resume life with her.

Six months after, Judah and Nubya moved into the house in St. John at the top of the climb that Judah's uncle had gifted him.

THREE TO ONE IS MURDER

Heading home from his meeting with Konjah Man, the sunlight cutting through the waking sky was bright enough to proclaim the full presence of daybreak. Judah stepped out onto the main road, where a track leading from the gully's floor to its mouth at the top ended.

He hadn't planned to be out this long. Having no desire to be seen heading home, Judah crossed the street and disappeared through some bushes. Only army men and a few monkey hunters knew this route. It was a path he would take on those days when he preferred to move incognito after finding himself exposed to broad daylight.

The heavy dew the night before had drenched the earth, making his footsteps mute under his weight. Eclipsed from the daylight, Judah walked through the woods that were populated primarily by mature river tamarinds. The cool, moist air carried the freshness of the morning. Dew sliding down the leaves from vines entangled within the trees dripped onto Judah's bare arms as he briskly made his way through.

From what he had seen earlier of the sun's position, Judah calculated that he should arrive home around seven. Konjah Man and Zaire would reach at eight, then he and Nubya could clear out by nine o'clock to head over to Marley's for breakfast.

Judah never understood the whole leaving home to go eat breakfast at someone else's house, when he could easily put on a cup of tea and down some fruits at his own home and call that *that*. But Marley was fancy. She made an occasion out of everything, from sunrises to sunsets, and all that could happen in between them. For her, life was one big event.

Halfway along his journey, Judah felt unsure about something. His five senses could not detect anything unusual. But of all his senses, he trusted his sixth the most. He stopped to listen to his surroundings, smell the air, and scan the shadows for signs that he should be wary of something ominous. But nothing manifested. Judah looked over his shoulders to see if he was being followed. Nothing.

Judah pressed on, but the feeling of uneasiness became overbearing. Alarmingly, his sixth sense rattled his body with such a wave of discomfort that he squatted down at the base of a grand cabbage palm that had exerted its dominance over the other trees around it. Its trunk was wide, which hid him from onlookers on the opposite side of the woods, if there were indeed any.

Judah still felt exposed. He scanned a patch of bamboo and saw nothing. He ran his eyes over the boughs of some nearby almond trees. *Nothing.* Spotting the leafy, low-hanging branches of a pair of junior clammacherry trees, he darted over to them and hid under their natural veil. Scoping out the landscape from the shroud their leaves provided, he still saw nothing.

His five senses remained unaffected, but Judah's sixth sense wouldn't hyper down. So Judah undressed. Hurriedly, he took off his tam and vest, carefully removed his gold chain from around his neck, and stripped the three gold rings from his right hand and two from his left. Then he placed everything in the center of his vest and rolled them up tightly. He quickly removed his boots, pants, and underwear. He added his rolled-up vest to the bundle and neatly stashed everything at the base of the trees, covering them with damp leaves.

Judah was stark naked. His sculpted body, etched from the demands of manual labor, was lean and gently defined. Confidently, his chest sat slightly raised above his carved washboard abs, set in a torso that flowed triangularly into his groin. Long, athletic legs, supported by strong, manly feet, carried his muscular body. Cascading down his broad back, Judah's thick, rope-like locs enveloped his frame, eventually dangling just below his mid-thigh. He was beautiful.

Getting down on his knees, Judah sat back on his heels. Centering himself, he tilted his head upward and opened his arms out to the side, tucking his elbows into his torso. He closed his eyes, opened his mouth wide to the heavens, and drew a deep inhale that summoned a force of nature known only to certain men. He was one of those men. The downward force of the air filled his chest to capacity, activating an energy surge that circulated through his body and exited from his energetic points.

On his exhale, Judah was no longer a man. It was the best he could do. Judah's father had begun to teach him the art of shifting his shape. But Judah was still young in the science when his father disappeared at sea. He never got the chance to master turning into anything more profound than a mongoose. Personally, he was fond of mongooses and would take on their shape on days such as these, when added discretion was needed.

Judah sniffed the air. He lowered himself onto all fours. Furry and barely two feet in length, he darted out from beneath the clammacherry trees. His tiny ears cocked, listening for unusual sounds in the woods. He hurriedly scampered from bush to bush, his beady, red eyes scanning the terrain for discrepancies.

The patch of woods came to an abrupt end. Judah scuttled through the grass and over some boulders to cut across the outer edges of the palings behind some of the village houses. He was finally in his district. His home was nearby.

But Judah's sixth sense was still agitated. He scurried past the back of a paling that led onto an open lot. Suddenly, out sprang three dogs! They missed his brown, slender body by a gross overshot. Startled, Judah looked back and hurled a ferocious hiss at the canines before running away in pursuit of safety.

There were three of them—mongrels—that looked like they all had no owners. The leader of the pack was an aggressive mixed breed with a horrid bark that elevated the dog's viciousness. Behind him was a mid-sized mutt that had mange along its front right leg and a poorly healed scar on its left shoulder. The animal looked like a victim of neglect.

By his side was the third dog, a pedigree pot-starver with a hollow bark, which looked eager to make a meal out of the mongoose.

They had all seen better days. But that didn't change the fact that mongoose and dog fights never end well for the runty mammal—no matter what. A mongoose and three dogs? Run!

Judah's tiny clawed feet moved as fast as adrenaline would allow them. His alert eyes gauged the approaching landscape as he dashed along the unkempt fringes of backyard palings, which quickly ended, bringing him head-on with a twenty-foot rock face. He was forced to make a ninety-degree left turn, which led him in the direction of the main road.

The barking intensified. Savagely, the three dogs followed, determined in their pursuit. Judah moved swiftly. Maneuvering nimbly through the grassy spaces had given him an advantage. But when he hit the open road to make the hundred-meter dash for the path that ran parallel to the steps leading up to his house, the canine predators began to gain ground.

"We gine kill you like rasshole!" the leader eerily barked from his frothing mouth.

As a mongoose, Judah could only understand the thoughts of his familiars. But here he was, picking up the thoughts of some random dog. Was this random? Nah. The only way he would be able to hear the thoughts of the dog, was if it, too, were a human in animal form, just like he was.

Judah sprinted up the side of the climb to his house as if the devil was after his soul. The barbaric sound of the pack's vicious barking was maniacal, shattering the serenity of everything within earshot. Pulling the climb siphoned off the stamina of the animals. The weaker dogs began to show signs of fatigue. Undeterred, the incense leader of the pack dug into the challenge.

Judah's mongoose form was halfway up the path when, unaware, he tripped over a freshly dug crab hole in the middle of the pathway. He lost his footing, stumbling in shock as the earth gave way under him on his bolt to freedom.

Judah's recovery was split second. He scurried to rebuild his pace. But the lead dog had already gained ground. He bound at Judah, planting a bite on the mongoose's hind. A primordial hiss escaped from Judah as he sprang forward to save himself from the imminent danger of being mauled to death. Excited by the success of the first blow, the two lagging dogs quickened their pace, barking expletives at Judah as they neared the top of the climb.

Judah's wrought iron gate was almost in reach by a mere few feet when the lead dog lunged out at him again. He landed a solid bite into Judah's leg, tearing the flesh. The connection instantly halted Judah. Coming to a sudden stop, the momentum from the chase left the alpha canine's body lurched over the injured mongoose.

Unable to move, Judah hissed defensively, slapping out at the predator lording over him. Surrounding the downed animal, the other dogs barked on malevolently, salivating through their growls as they made ready to end his life.

Aiming to slash their noses with his unsheathed claws, Judah slapped out at the dogs again. But he missed, and the lead dog pounced upon him. Grabbing Judah's grizzly body with his sharp teeth, the dog violently shook the mongoose's small frame. He raised Judah's body into the air. Just as he was about to smash Judah into the ground, a bullet pierced the mixed breed's side.

His grip loosened. His growl snapped into a yelp. The half-dead mongoose dropped from his jaws and thumped down onto the top step by the foot of the landing.

Nubya fired two more shots in the direction of the dogs, aiming one at each of the other mongrels. But they had already begun their retreat. In the frenzy to get away, the leader of the pack lost his balance and tumbled onto one of the other dogs, causing them both to roll to the bottom of the climb, unable to catch their footing. The sounds of animals in anguish pierced the heavens, then abruptly disappeared.

Nubya opened the gate and stepped around the mongoose to head down the steps to inspect the scene. Reaching the bottom, she found a pool of blood by the side of the road, but no signs of the dogs in any which direction.

Realizing her hand was shaking, she put the safety lock back on the gun. Unsettled, Nubya languidly made her way back up the climb. She always secretly loved the scent of gunpowder. But mixed with the scent of pierced flesh, it made her stomach sick.

Returning home, at the midway point as Nubya rounded the slight bend in the climb, she spotted the bloodied naked body of a man lying on the landing at the entrance to her gate. It was her husband, Judah.

16

YOU NAKED THOUGH

"I like I can't change back!" Bewilderment took over the mid-sized mutt after tumbling down the climb. The burning force from the bullet piercing the chest deflated the actions of the pack's leader. He felt his life leaving him unexpectedly as his lungs collapsed, defeated by the murderous intruder.

Everything was spinning, even after he landed on top of the mid-sized mutt, depositing his full mass upon his subordinate. The pot-starver had changed back to his rakey, downtrodden human form. But his colleague still resembled a canine.

"Wuh you mean you can't change back? You mad or wuh?" he demanded of the mutt standing in front of him projecting whimpers of disbelief. "How I suppose to move he?" the rakey one asked, signaling across in the direction of their leader, whom the momentum of the tumble had hurtled from the foot of the climb onto the curb of the street. His convulsing body, which rapidly transitioned back to its human form upon the impact of the bullet, now spasmed as he catched for breath, to no avail.

Grumbling with dissatisfaction, the lone man shot the mutt a stink look and proceeded over to his superior.

"Pssst. Pssst. My man, duck down. You naked, though," the mutt found it necessary to bring to his partner's attention.

"Yes, I am naked. And you are still a dog. Now that we are done with the obvious, let's go."

He snatched the body up as best he could, hoisting its limpness over his left shoulder with the upper half of the form dangling down his back. Across his torso hung two scruffy scar-imprinted legs, which he gripped to keep the body steady.

"You wait," he grumbled under his breath as he crossed the road. Bypassing the first two houses he encountered, he made a sharp entry through a slim opening where their boundaries met. He then proceeded through to a tiny path that led up to a bigger path that eventually deposited him onto a cart road. The whole time, he grumbled. Acid about the counterattack, he brimmed with angst.

"You wait. Dem feel it going finish so? You wait," he repeated the mantra, fuming at his present condition. Bloodied and naked in the streets, carrying dead weight over his shoulder, his mission was incomplete.

The morning sun had changed from charming to cutting. Blood drained from the foreign body to tangle in with its carrier's sweat, making it hard to transport the load on his now slippery shoulder.

Stopping in the middle of the cart road, he laid the nude

corpse on the rocky ground, assessed the scene before him, then hastily departed. The naked man and his dog, cutting through the bush, made their escape.

17

A PARADE OF CLOUDS

"Come quickly! I don't know what to do!" Nubya cried into her cell phone.

Marley was in the middle of a live broadcast when Nubya called, frantic. Marley had spent the night at her family's rental property and was chatting to her following about the importance of taking time out for one's self. She had gone down to the shore to share the sunrise with her followers, telling them about the cleanliness and reviving freshness of the Atlantic Ocean air.

The family property sat on the beachfront. The house had a back gate that directly opened onto the sand. Marley had teased her social media followers that she couldn't be at every event, every weekend, and advised them of the importance of tending to their relationships—whether with friends, family, or self. In a bit, she would be making breakfast for her clan and wanted everyone to join her for that broadcast, at which point, she would demonstrate the art of loving up your bona fides, culinary style.

Nubya rang Marley's phone. She didn't answer.

"I'm starting the day off by preparing breakfast for my people. Then, we'll probably hit the beach after that. In the comments section below, tell me what your plans are for today. Remember, whatever you do, do it with love. One love, every time." Marley abruptly ended the live broadcast to answer her friend, who was ringing her mobile phone repeatedly, which was odd.

"They hurt Judah! I don't know what to do!"

"Hurt how? Who are *they*?" Marley asked Nubya as she hurriedly went indoors, no longer feeling to be outside after ending her live broadcast.

"He's bleeding …" Nubya faded.

"Bleeding? How bad? What happened?" Marley asked while she searched for her keys. Marley was met with silence.

When Nubya found him on the ground outside of the house, Judah's skin glistened in the patches where ruby red blood was escaping from his body. The chipper chirps and raucous crowing that sprang the day to life grated on her nerves. She needed silence in the worst way so she could process the sight that lay before her.

Upset. Unsure. Lost. Not a single tear mounted in her eyes. Nubya rushed to Judah's side, bent over him, resting her forehead on his cheek. His skin was ablaze. Pressing her trembling lips into his flesh, she inhaled him. He smelled otherworldly. The tears began to flow.

This day was as familiar to her as all the moments prior, which she had replayed repeatedly in her head whenever she entertained fears that, someday, she could tragically lose him. The emptiness was heavier than she expected it to be. Death was finally at her door.

"Nubya," Marley repeated, "you there? Nubya?" She

raised her voice, frustrated at not being able to find her keys so she could leave the house to be with her friend. "Hang up. I'm going to video call you so you can show me what's happened."

Marley called back right away. When Nubya answered the video call, Marley could see Judah lying bloodied on the ground.

"Is he naked? Why is he naked?" Marley finally found something to say. "Go inside and get a sheet and cover him," she urged. "Nubya! You hear me?"

Nubya looked into the phone, bewildered. Her face shimmering from the mix of tears and snot running down its surface.

Marley lowered her tone, slowed her words, and urged her friend again. "Go inside and get a sheet to cover his body. You understand me?"

This time, Nubya set the phone on the ground, leaving Marley to watch a parade of clouds floating across the sky. Nubya returned and picked up the phone again.

"Is he alive?" Marley asked.

Nubya nodded, trembled, then burst into a fresh set of tears.

"Nubya. I'm on my way," Marley assured, having finally found her keys. She started her vehicle and headed out of the driveway.

"Bella, Bella. I don't want to leave you, but I have to hang up to make some calls. You overs?" Marley queried to the silence at the other end. "Nubya, you understand me? Say something!"

Nubya nodded and let a trembling finger end the call. Just as Marley was about to call I-Am, I-Am rang Marley.

"I-Am, something bad has happened to Judah," Marley reported.

"Wait. I can't hear you properly," I-Am responded, repositioning her phone as she headed into the next room in search of better reception. "You can hear me?"

"Yes. Can you hear me?" Marley replied.

"Yeah."

"Something bad has happened to Judah."

"What?"

"I'm on my way over there now. I don't know the fullness of what has happened. Can you, Zaire, and Shotta meet me at Nubya's?"

"Shotta! Shotta! Come quick!" I-Am called out to the background in the middle of her and Marley's conversation. "Shotta, where you is? Shotta, you outside?" I-Am questioned loudly as she moved through the house, trying to locate her brother.

"I here on the phone with Marley," her voice finally lowered. "She's on her way to Nubya. Something bad happened to Judah!" I-Am explained to her brother.

"What! Bad like wuh? He dead?" Marley could hear Shotta's response questions.

"He dead?" I-Am returned to her conversation with Marley.

"He nearly look it. All I saw is that he's outside, lying down in a pool of blood, and Nubya's head gone," Marley recounted.

In the background, Shotta instructed I-Am, "Wait. Put she pun speaker," then to Marley said, "Marley, what is that you say?"

"He nearly look like he's dead. I don't know. I can't really tell. All I saw is that he's outside lying down in a pool of blood, and Nubya's head is gone."

"Sis, we heading 'cross there now. Zaire! Fall in!" The phone cut out in Marley's ear. A few minutes later, she pulled into the parking spot at the front of Ms. Ashby's shop. Getting out of the vehicle, Marley spotted a pool of blood a few feet away.

Some neighbors were outside, looking more like loiters than active members of the community. Not one of them dared to venture up to the shop, nor even near the steps to investigate the strange noises or the gunshots. Instead, they all waited. Somebody of merit was bound to turn up soon because a pool of blood sat in the street, which meant police, or ambulance, or both would soon appear, and things would have to come out.

18

ZAIRE

Marley jumped out of her truck and sprinted up the steps of the climb. The site of Nubya slumped over Judah's partially mauled body was something Marley was not prepared for.

From where she stood, a few steps away, he looked dead. Timidly, she approached the couple, not knowing what to expect.

"Dogs!" Nubya whimpered.

"Dogs?" Marley repeated, surveying the fullness of what lay before her as she crouched down cautiously by Nubya's side.

"Bella, why is he naked?" Marley asked, concerned.

"Dogs," Nubya replied, welling up with tears again.

"I don't understand."

Nubya said nothing.

"We have to take him to the hospital," Marley reasoned.

"No ..." Soft like a puff of smoke, Nubya had released the unexpected response into the air. "No!" she repeated a little stronger than before, in hopes of making sure that Marley understood.

Marley was beat. "Nubya, he can't stay here bleeding out like this. You'll lose him."

"No!"

Just then, a gallop of footsteps came rushing up the climb. Shotta Forward was a big man. Six-feet, five-inches tall, weighing no less than 300 pounds; however, he carried his weight with the agility of a ballerino. With him were Zaire and Konjah Man. I-Am was a little ways behind them, with one hand under her pregnant belly as she came up the steps.

The site of their slain brethren halted them all. I-Am cupped her face, then spat the bad taste from her mouth. Konjah Man found his words first.

"That is Judah blood down there in the road?" Konjah Man asked.

Something clicked and Nubya found herself for a moment.

"No. It's the dog's. I shot one of them," Nubya informed as she sat up to face her friends. The only problem with her story was that there was no sign of dogs anywhere.

From by her side, Nubya pulled out the gun that had laid hidden under her skirt while she wept. Everyone was immediately startled. Konjah Man came forward, walked past Marley and Judah, approached Nubya, and gently took the gun from her svelte hand in one swift motion.

"We can figure this out later. But he got to get to a hospital now!" Shotta suggested passionately.

"Daughter, we need to see his wounds," Konjah Man

pleaded with Nubya as he handed her gun to Shotta Forward.

Marley carefully pulled back the sheet, half exposing his body. Zaire and Shotta came forward to get a closer look. The urgency of the situation was clear. Judah was in bad shape and needed a doctor's care immediately. But then, Nubya burst out and started talking like a possessed woman at confession.

"I heard the dogs outside, making real nuff noise. It woke me up. Judah wasn't here. The noise was far off. Far, far. But then, it kept coming closer and closer. These dogs sounded possessed. They were making me angry 'cause I was trying to sleep," Nubya said.

"I grabbed the gun and headed outside 'cause what pissed me off even more was that I heard them sounding like they were coming up the steps to the house. Why were they bringing that ruckus to our door? You know how wild dogs are when you see them behaving like that?" she continued.

"I grabbed the gun, came outside, fired a shot, and hit one. Then, I fired again but missed the other two. When I reached the gate, I saw a mongoose lying on the step like dem was chasing de poor thing and was about to kill it. I saw that the dogs were gone. Not a sign of them up here. But I wanted to make sure. So I went down to the bottom. But I ain't see no sign of the dogs down there, neither. Just de pool of blood," Nubya explained.

"When I get back up the steps, I see Judah lying here, naked, where the mongoose had been. Bleeding. Just so naked and bleeding." Nubya teared up again.

"What de fuck you telling me?" Zaire blurted out each word with emphasis.

Everybody was thinking it.

"We can't go to no hospital 'cause you know Judah and Babylon don't 'gree," Marley offered.

"Wait! So wunna gine act like she ain't just say what she just say?" Zaire questioned the group.

"Zaire!" I-Am snapped. She took two deep draws from her Vicks inhaler and repeated the motion for added effect.

"What de fuck she telling we I-yah?" Zaire asked as he backed away from the scene, shaking his head in disbelief.

Marley still had her phone and keys gripped in her hand. She began dialing a number. She ended the phone call by saying, "We are on our way now."

PART III

19

HOLD THE ORDER

Monday morning was dreadful. A sleep-deprived Marley opened her morning radio show with Junior X's serious tune, "Plead My Cause," continuing down that line of messaging for the entirety of her five-hour shift.

Halfway through, when Shotta Forward turned up at the station to co-host his sponsored segment, Marley gave him an extended hug, reluctant to leave the security of his large frame. DJ Kutlass sensed that something was up but refrained from inquiring. Uncertainty about the day's energy left Zoe acting fidgety. Whenever the "On-Air" button went off, barely a word was spoken by anyone.

The morning in front, Shotta Forward wrapped Judah's body in a second sheet. He lifted Judah's limp form down the climb and placed him in his pickup truck. Marley and Nubya rode with Shotta Forward to the location of the person on the other line. Both women sat in the leather backseat of the vehicle, lending support to Judah's body from either side.

At the house, Konjah Man and Zaire went into the drying room and divided the Bajan Green between two black garbage bags. They then placed each bag in a crocus shopping bag that carried the name of Nubya's favorite farmers' co-op brightly printed across the sides.

Zaire scrubbed down the bloodied steps with Cloroxed water. He showered the area with diluted Jeyes Fluid, then proceeded to wash away the drying pool of blood down by the roadside. It sent a stream of stained water racing toward the village, until it eventually ran clear.

I-Am packed a suitcase of personal items for Nubya and Judah. Then, with Konjah Man's help, she swept the house clean, leaving not even an herb seed to be found. I-Am turned on two strategic lights inside the house and activated the outdoor light sensor that would cause the yard lights to come on when triggered by any motion outside of the house. When they were done, they locked up and headed out.

Loudly colorful synthetic curtains concealed curious faces, strategically positioned behind louvered windows, trying to catch a glimpse of the clandestine activity. Closed doors restrained occupants from giving in to the urge to rush out onto the street and inevitably create a spectacle out of the morning's calamity.

Judah was that kind of man. He commanded that level of respect. No one dared to make a scene out of the situation. Not even if they wanted to.

Suspicious neighbors watched on as Zaire, Konjah Man, and I-Am packed into the double cab of Marley's Mitsubishi L200 and left. I-Am dropped Zaire off at his home, which was a few houses down the gap from where she lived. He took the crocus shopping bags with him.

Konjah Man, who had ridden his bicycle over to Judah's that morning, removed it from the pickup's cargo bed and leaned it up along the side of Zaire's house, giving the appearance as if he were there visiting. He followed Zaire through the side gate, leading into the backyard. There, he privately gave instructions for how to handle matters in his, Judah's, and Shotta Forward's absence.

Zaire was still in disbelief. The story that Nubya told meant that she had either gone crazy or was telling the truth —neither of which consoled Zaire any.

Zaire had seen blood before. Cleaned it up, too. He was a fighter. Cockfights and, at times, dogfights, were his thing. The latter was the messier of the two, though. Cleaning up after a bad dogfight either broke you down, or eventually numbed you to the gruesomeness of the carnage. Zaire was nowhere near broken. He had seen many fighters defeated or injured in battle. However, the sight of his boss lying naked on the ground—unconscious, mauled, and bloodied—was a first.

Zaire always kept his surroundings immaculately clean. The chicken pens in his backyard were a neatly constructed roost for his fighter stock. Each coop housed either a known winner or a rising star.

By the time Zaire reached back home that morning, his cousin Tommy had already started to sun the partially plucked birds on the thick cable that was affixed to two wooden poles, a few feet out behind Zaire's yard. Tommy had just finished tying the last of the birds to the line. He would leave them perched there so the morning sun could bathe the areas of exposed skin—warrior patches from previous fights—in need of the healing delivered by the nutrient-rich morning sunlight.

Tommy returned to the yard in time to catch Konjah Man's departing words to Zaire as he headed back out through the side gate to leave with I-Am.

"Hold the order."

20

THE CENOTE

Shotta Forward's Navara tore down the road leading up to Lee Mile's house, inadvertently tossing around the occupants in the backseat. Lee Mile was already outside when Shotta pulled up. Seeing that the front passenger seat was empty, Lee Mile made his approach to the door behind it.

Pulling it open, he stood face-to-face with a terror-stricken Nubya. In her arms was Judah's limp body, wrapped in blood-stained sheets. Over at the opposite end of the seat Marley looked on ready to make something happen. Lee Mile registered the entire scene before Shotta Forward could exit the driver's side of the pickup.

"Don't get out," Lee Mile instructed as he closed the back door and took up a position in the front passenger seat.

"Follow that road across there." He pointed to a cart road that led further onto his property.

Shotta Forward followed the instructions. Marley, sensing that there were things Lee Mile needed to know, began to recount Nubya's story to him about the dogs. "So, I called you 'cause we can't take this situation to no hospital. They would put her in the mental or lock her up!"

"Cut through there," Lee Mile continued, guiding Shotta Forward.

Up to this point, Marley had recognized the orchards, the pond, some pasture areas, but this part of the property was unfamiliar to her.

Shifting the position of the chewstick that protruded slightly from the left corner of his mouth, Lee Mile cautioned Shotta Forward to take it easy.

"Turn through there," Lee Mile indicated. The openness of the landscape started to diminish, forcing Shotta Forward to cautiously navigate the fading cart road. Eventually, Shotta was forced to slow down. For a second, sizing up the woods ahead of him, he wondered if his truck would be able to squeeze through the narrow opening.

"What you does call out here?" Shotta Forward questioned.

"St. Andrew," Lee Mile replied, shutting down the conversation.

The path ended abruptly at a wall of woods that showed no sign that there was anything beyond it. So Shotta Forward stopped the vehicle. Marley looked on, puzzled, confused as to why Lee Mile had them out in the middle of the bush and not at his house attending to Judah. Nubya, helpless, was lost for words.

"Drive. Straight ahead," Lee Mile commanded. He began to run his hands down each opposite arm, across his face, and over his chest.

"Big man," Shotta Forward replied, "I ain't taking my truck through that," referencing the densely wooded area in front of them with no visible track for driving.

Marley jumped in on a leap of faith. "Shotta, just do it. Please. I don't understand either. If it comes to it, I will fix whatever needs fixing after. But for Judah's sake, listen to Lee Mile and drive. Please," she pleaded.

Reluctantly, Shotta Forward started to drive, inching the vehicle forward. Mysteriously, a hidden path opened up and revealed itself. Directly up ahead stood the largest silk cotton tree that any of them had ever seen. It was in bloom. Towering upward like a skyscraper, everything below it was covered in the soft, cotton-like fluff that the tree released from the numerous fruit pods dangling from its branches.

The sight looked like a winter wonderland, but in the tropics and, thankfully, without the cold weather. The soft, silky puffs from the tree floated through the air, landing upon everything within reach. Everyone was enchanted by the tree's glory. But Lee Mile kept his focus.

Shotta Forward was certain he was driving. The truck's speedometer indicated that the vehicle was moving. But, from the looks of it, his surroundings were not. Testing his theory, Shotta Forward sped up a little. He slowed down some. But the silk cotton tree remained visibly the same distance away no matter what he did.

"Lee Mile, what's happening?" Marley asked, realizing they were literally going nowhere fast.

Nubya began to weep.

"Stop here," Lee Mile commanded.

As soon as Shotta Forward stopped the vehicle, the

surrounding woods changed position. The silk cotton tree was now behind them, but no one recalled having ever passed it.

"Let's get him inside. We are working with very little time," Lee Mile advised.

Shotta Forward exited the vehicle and came around to help Nubya out of the backseat. Her top was bloodstained. The snot and tears had partially dried on her face, leaving her looking like an infant whose crying face hadn't been wiped. Marley attempted to pry Judah out of Nubya's arms.

"You have to let him go, or else we can't save him. You hear me?" Marley coaxed her friend.

Shotta Forward leaned in and lifted Nubya out of the vehicle. Marley propped Judah's torso up against the seat, then scurried around the back of the pickup. She grabbed Nubya by the waist in an attempt to support her footing. Shotta Forward reached back into the backseat and secured Judah's lean frame in his arms.

"Bring him this way," Lee Mile said as he started to walk ahead of them.

No one could figure out where they were or where they were going. The woods were an illusion. That, they were sure of. Nothing was what it seemed nor where it seemed to be. It was all too dizzying for the newcomers. The only person who seemed certain of anything's location was Lee Mile. So, obediently, they followed on.

The group came to a stately bearded fig tree with a collection of huge, naturally formed archways in its trunk. Reaching down to the earth, projectiles of aerial roots at different stages of maturity dangled from the tree's branches.

Exiting out of a dimly lit archway, through to the other side, they found themselves in a sunny clearing of about thirty feet wide. The cenote had a wall of raw limestone, ten feet in height, that formed a perimeter around the circumference. On top of it, mature bearded fig trees sprawled out and towered up, enclosing the space.

In the bosom of the clearing sat an emerald blue pool, fed by trickling streams spilling over the limestone rock's face and washing down into its waters. At the base of the limestone wall, a second block of limestone about two feet wide jutted out over the water below like a shelf, which allowed the brave of heart to walk fully around the pool.

The archway deposited Marley and her friends a few feet from the pool's entrance. At its mouth, shallow slabs of rocks leading down into the pool formed a natural entry point into the body of water that glistened strikingly from the light entering the clearing from overhead.

There were so many questions to be asked, but no one dared to utter a word. Even Nubya seemed to have found herself again in this mystical place.

"Take off your shoes and walk straight into the water, all the way to the midway point. Make sure to keep his body submerged," Lee Mile guided Shotta Forward. "I'm going to have to relieve you of your guns, though."

Shotta was compliant and did as instructed, allowing Lee Mile to remove the weapons from his waist.

Emerging from out of an archway of the tree that they had just passed through, Marley recognized the young woman from the night before who had served her soup at Lee Mile's gathering. She was dressed in a white, silk cotton kaftan. Cradled in her left arm, she carried a bundle of bush as she played a rhythm on a pair of calabash rattles in her right hand.

Lee Mile took the bundle and placed it on the ground in front of him. He opened it up and removed two ceramic jars as everyone looked on, Nubya and Marley standing awkwardly by the entrance, Shotta Forward immersed in the warm mineral pool, standing with Judah's body draped across his arms.

Shotta Forward stared down at Judah, suspended in his grip. The sparkling water lapping at the flaccid body of his brethren. He felt helpless. No one knew what was going on, but no one had any other alternative. So they continued to keep quiet.

Shotta looked up to take a peek at the sky. When he looked back down again, Lee Mile was standing before him, slightly higher than waist-deep in the water.

Lee Mile unwrapped the sheets covering Judah and gave them to the young woman, who was now standing behind him, still rhythmically shaking the calabash rattles.

It was the first time they all saw the fullness of the damage to Judah's body. The gash down his leg. The bite marks. The broken ribs from being shaken. His eyes half-cocked in unconsciousness, mouth crooked, face frozen with a grimace. Judah's locs, hovering around his dome, floated like tentacles as they reached out into the pool, as if in communion with the water.

No one knew when the chanting began. No one knew how they knew the words to the songs or where the extra voices that joined them came from. Who were those people sitting at the feet of the surrounding trees like angels dressed in white? The drumming? The calls of the men? The responses of the women? What about that strange scent the two elders released into the air from the burning sticks they carried? There was no recollection of when the bloodied water turned crystal blue again, or of how much time had gone by. Everything just *happened*.

Lee Mile finally broke the spell. Nubya saw it first. The blinking of Judah's eyes. His consciousness returning. They all huddled around him with expectation as he lay upon a coconut fiber mattress, surrounded by unfamiliar ornate objects and concoctions.

Marley became aware that they were now inside of a large clearing within a huge above-ground root structure of an elderly bearded fig tree. Lee Mile had just finished applying some kind of ochre-colored ointment to Judah's body, on top of which he strategically placed fiber-based bandages.

The young woman with the calabash rattles was kneeling over Judah's head, with one hand circling his temples. Her lips moved, but no words came out. She was eyeing each of the room's occupants. Directly engaging their stares as she looked past them. She appeared to be talking *to* them, but not *with* them.

Shotta Forward, coming to his senses, patted down his body and felt for the guns, which he found lodged in the waist of his pants against his back. How was it that he was now dry? Was he not just waist deep in a pool of water? Marley looked around. She saw everything but nothing at all.

The young woman arose from her post and removed her hand from over Judah's head. Bringing her rhythmic rattling to an end, she looked across in Shotta Forward's direction and sent an intention his way. He received it. Obediently, he arose and followed her through an archway that led out of the room.

21

THE AMAZONIAN GIANT

Nubya and Marley sporadically exchanged mixed looks as they watched each application of care Lee Mile used to restore life to Judah. Applying the last piece of dressing, when Lee Mile finished attending to Judah's body, he sealed off the process with what felt like an ancient prayer. A force of energy rushed through the grand bearded fig tree's archways, washing over the room's occupants. It proceeded to climb the walls of roots surrounding the inhabitants, then hovered above them in the healing chamber where Judah rested.

The tentacle-like root structure of the hollow space radiated a warm luminance that traveled from the soil, along the root canal, and up to the broad trunk of the tree. The effulgence from the energy's journey allowed the occupants to see with the clearness of day in the absence of it being daytime.

The chamber seemed in sync with Judah's life force. It pulsed in a syncopating manner, similar to the faint rhythm that lifted and lowered Judah's chest as he breathed.

"He is young in the science," Lee Mile gently explained to Marley and Nubya as his eyes roved the faces of the two women seated clustered on the other side of the mattress where Judah lay. "Life is about forces. This man knows the science of those forces, as well as he doesn't know it," Lee Mile continued on while shifting his chewstick to a more secure location in the left corner of his mouth as he spoke.

"Stop. I'm confused. Where did she take Shotta?" Marley asked, hurriedly trying to patch together the pieces of all that had transpired. Marley felt like she was tumbling down from a horrible psychedelic mushroom trip; yet, she still had her wits about her. Shotta Forward had exited with the mysterious woman, without saying a word to any of them. Where was the explanation?

"To prepare him for what is to happen next," Lee Mile responded assuredly.

"What is to happen next? Like what, Lee Mile? All of this is a bit much. I thank you from the depths of my soul for preserving Judah's life. But please, for the love of Jah, explain what is going on here. Don't get me wrong. This far exceeds anything I could have envisioned when I reached out to you for help with Judah. But that said, I don't know what to make of any of this," Marley vented.

Through it all, Nubya hadn't taken her eyes off Judah from her position next to the mattress, where he lay recovering. She wasn't sure what to do nor what to think. Was he really alive? His eyes flickered sporadically behind closed lids. The grimace on his face from earlier had crawled away into nothingness, leaving behind the structural beauty of the man she loved and almost lost.

She was scared to touch him, reluctant for the hotness of

her curiosity to meet the possibility of the cold flesh of a lover gone. Could she touch him, though? Smeared in ointment. Wrapped in bandages. His locs piled in a lifeless bundle next to his shoulder. He looked so frail. If he did make it through, how was she to care for him? The accumulation of his life battles seemed to be escaping through his pores, pouring out in convoys of sweat along his body. How bad was he damaged? Would they leave this place, and when they did, where would they go?

"Give thanks." Nubya cut across Marley's venting to adorn Lee Mile with her gratitude. She shifted the weight of her tam, adjusting her hair as she looked up at Lee Mile. "Give thanks for saving his life."

Fresh tears sprang forth from the corners of Nubya's eyes. She cupped her face in the same delicate hands that had earlier shot Judah's assailant. Marley gathered her friend into a consoling embrace.

"Your husband will live. He will heal. He will remember," Lee Mile explained. "You will remember, too, but you must forget. Leave him with his mysteries. Let him have his private life. He will stay here for a few days, as will you. Because of who he is, his recovery will manifest differently from that of a typical man. I mean that in a good way."

Lee Mile nodded in acknowledgment of Nubya's offering of thanks. He arose from Judah's side and proceeded to exit through an archway, leaving the two women to process the moment alone.

A while later, Lee Mile returned, cleaned up. He wore a fresh change of clothes. A chocolate-colored guayabera shirt with tan embroidering, cargo pants, and his signature mocha-colored push-up front Amica leather sandals. Standing at the entrance of the chamber, for a brief moment, his skin seemed to match the glow of his surroundings. A woodsy aroma emanating from his body gradually perfumed the space where they were gathered, leaving a slight undertone of musk fragrance lingering in the air.

Marley sat with Nubya, huddled together by Judah's side on a pair of Senufo stools. At the sound of Lee Mile's presence, they both looked up. Lee Mile paused at the entrance. He measured the anticipation in Nubya's eyes while he registered a question being forged as Marley began to frame her sentence.

"You know what happens when you step on a centipede?" Lee Mile asked his audience as he eyed the scene before him.

"What?" Marley responded, rising from Nubya's side to look Lee Mile straight in his face.

"Do you know what happens when you step on a centipede to kill it?" he repeated, fixing his gaze on Nubya as he turned away from Marley. She could feel his dominance fill the room as it searched out the answer.

Marley scanned Lee Mile's face in disbelief. Where was this line of questioning coming from? She tried to connect with his eyes, but they paid her no attention. Instead, they looked down at Nubya, seated at her husband's side, staring off into the thoughts that raced across her mind.

"Nubya, do you know what happens when you step on a centipede?" Lee Mile now directed his question straight at her.

Nubya's gaze climbed up to meet Lee Mile's probing

stare. The silence between them chilled the room. Marley had never seen this side of Lee Mile. Who was this man who stood before her with the better part of six inches of a centipede on his face?

Marley caught herself between blinks. The chewstick protruding out of Lee Mile's mouth was now a coal-black Amazonian giant centipede. As thick as a man's thumb, scores of writhing red legs extended from its anatomy, wrestling to escape the grip enforced by Lee Mile's ivory white teeth pressing down on a section of its elongated metameric body.

Dangling from the left corner of Lee Mile's mouth, the front portion of the determined centipede desperately clawed at the air, while dozens more legs pricked into the soft flesh of Lee Mile's scowling lips. Sensing the heat from his skin, the carnivorous Amazonian contorted its spineless body. Doubling back, it collapsed onto Lee Mile's face with a multitude of legs clawing for a firm grip of Lee Mile's jaw, in hopes of prying free.

Marley froze at the scene before her. The black predator, with its cavalry of fiery legs, finding it difficult to hold onto Lee Mile's face, erected its segmented body into an attack stance. Lee Mile swiftly bit down, splitting the centipede's body in two before it could launch its venomous strike. The Amazonian giant centipede, landing belly up, revealing a yellow underside, immediately flipped right side up just as it hit the floor.

In full attack mode, the centipede raced toward Nubya who, up until that moment, was still seated on the Senufo stool, stricken from the grotesque sight playing out in front of her.

The crazed centipede's sprint in Nubya's direction caused her to jump up in fear. Nubya quickly grabbed the stool that was next to her and drove one of its wooden legs into the wriggling body of the attacking arthropod. She barely connected with the creature but managed to pin a portion of the bloodcurdling predator to the ground.

Do you know what happens if you step on a centipede? A vicious warrior, the Amazonian reared up its unpinned head, bringing along with it whatever portion of his segmented body that was free. He buckled back, driving a venomous attack sting into the leg of the stool. Instinctively, Nubya quickly lifted the stool and in a pile-driving motion, faster than the Amazonian could think to make his next move, she hit the centipede again. This time, crushing it flat.

"The dogs you speak of, Nubya, they are men." While Lee Mile spoke, the remaining half of the centipede crawled out of his mouth and hung onto the left corner of Lee Mile's face. Grabbing at his chin. Searching for its missing body.

"One of them will die. The others will live out their lives afflicted, but not before attempting to cause you great harm," Lee Mile warned. As he spoke, the portion of centipede that rummaged across Lee Mile's face from its perch on the left corner of his mouth disappeared. In its place, Lee Mile was repositioning his chewstick.

"Stinga has hurt for you in his heart. There is something at your house that these men are after. Where is it?" Lee Mile probed.

Marley cocked her head to the side and took a look at Nubya, as if seeing her for the first time. Nubya broke her silence.

"Judah has it stashed at the top of the coconut tree."

22

TEMPLE YARD

After her shift was over, Marley headed across to Temple Yard to have lunch at Vital Too with I-Am. It had only been three years ago that siblings, Shotta Forward and I-Am, opened their second Ital restaurant at its current location, in the heart of the capital, Bridgetown. The original Vital was based in St. John, in a two-story annex next to Shotta Forward's home.

Shotta Forward's foray into the restaurant business was completely accidental, born out of the realization that there was nowhere on his side of the island where he could consistently partake of genuine Rasta food—Ital. Yes, there were non-vegetarian establishments, claiming to cook authentic veg dishes in their meat kitchens. But Shotta Forward always had a feeling that the care needed to properly separate the demands required of the two styles of culinary arts wasn't always present or enforced at a level that made him 100 percent certain that the mindfulness needed for its preparation was always applied.

One day he ordered veg rice from one such establishment, only to find a salted pigtail—which traditionally is added to rice for flavor—sitting at the bottom of his container, Shotta Forward knew that his intuition was right. He stopped eating out altogether. Instead, he made the decision to allot a dedicated block of time each day to knox a pot so he would never be a victim of that type of deception again.

Shotta Forward was never about block life; though some would say his home attracted that kind of vibe. He had a natural magnetism that drew people in. On top of that, he was a fantastic host. People were always stopping by and seldom seemed inclined to leave in any hurry.

Sometimes they would stay so long that hunger would set in from the hours of liming, conversation, card playing, watching movies and, of course, partaking of herb. So being a hospitable man, Shotta Forward would knox a huge pot of food and feed whomever stopped by. His policy: the food was free; drinks, on the other hand, you had to buy.

Turns out Shotta Forward was quite gifted in the culinary arts. In five years, Shotta Forward was selling both food and drinks. His success placed him in a position to open a well-appointed restaurant that served Ital and vegetarian renditions of Caribbean Creole dishes. He made the staples that everyone knew and loved but kept things interesting by freshening up the menu with new dishes to mark different seasons and holidays.

Vital was simply an Irie place to be. It carried a polished, rustic roots vibe that was very welcoming. It was as if you had stepped into a Rastaman's home and were eating straight from his pot.

Along with ample seating for socializing, there was a bar, outdoor hearth, deck, and pool table. Unlike most cookshops, Vital was open from breakfast to dinner. Sometimes it seemed as if Vital never closed. Reggae music was constantly on rotation. Something was always cooking, and people were always there, ready to eat.

When Shotta Forward identified Bridgetown as the second location for Vital, Temple Yard was the automatic choice for Vital Too. Temple Yard was the largest Rastafari marketplace on the island. Regarded as iconic for half a century, Temple Yard was heralded as the heartbeat of Rastafari activity in the core of the city. Everyone rated it as the go-to place for Rastafari sculpture, arts and crafts, fashion, jewelry, leather goods, and, of course, food.

As good as it all sounded, with its rich history, prime location, and a collection of amazing artisans—Temple Yard, the authentic Rastafari culture market—as a place for commerce based on culture, its performance was underwhelming, haphazard, and disorganized on its best day.

Coming in as a potential tenant, Shotta Forward soon learned some hidden truths. The community water bill hadn't been paid in years, so the water that serviced the market had been disconnected long ago. The electricity, as well. Contrary to the governing covenants, gradually, instead of commercial spaces, many of the tenants had started to convert their shops into makeshift homes. Added to all of that, gang activity began to emerge within the Yard's quarters.

As disheartening as it all sounded, for some reason, these challenges did not diminish Shotta Forward's goal of opening Vital Too in Temple Yard. It was undeniable that the Yard was brimming with potential. Vital Too would still happen, but not before order was brought to the operations of the market.

On his first attempt to establish such order, Shotta Forward locked heads with ones who had long ago laid claim to the Yard. They were not keen on Shotta Forward disrupting their way of doing things. Shotta Forward had little desire to be patient with the situation. He wasn't about a bunch of long talk either. He knew most of the ones who operated in the space socially. But now, on a business level, he was relearning them. It was time for a change.

Shotta Forward decided to venture down a path led by diplomacy. He told himself he'd give the bredren over at the Yard three strikes, at most. On the eve of strike number four, Shotta Forward brought out his soldiers and raided Temple Yard.

Not the BDF, task force, nor police, as was customary. No, not Babylon, which would routinely shake down the place, looking for herb and the occasional outlaw. Nah. This time around, and most likely for the first time ever, a Rootsman raided the Yard. Determined to install a new order, Shotta Forward and his soldiers from the Revolutionary Action Syndicate shook the whole place up and shut everything down.

Tenants who hadn't paid rent in years, those who were misusing their shop spaces, ones who had failed to effectively handle the administration of the market's business—all were ousted. Not to be forgotten, those who thought that gangsta life would take hold of the Yard, quickly learned otherwise.

Shotta Forward's actions literally became the talk around town. He formed a new alliance with the ones who remained, creating committees and delegating tasks, all in a drive to push things forward. Together, the small collective succeeded in drafting up a master plan for Temple Yard. They embarked upon dialogue with stakeholders and community investors. They did so in hopes of opening up the Yard to other progressive ones who wanted in on the new vision of the Temple Yard culture market.

It took Shotta Forward and his collective a total of three years to fully actualize on their new vision for Temple Yard. From innovations in infrastructure to green initiatives, self-governance to sustainability, livity, and order, the Yard was expanded, spreading its operation to the reaches of its boundaries. It was then subdivided into four main sections. One for each mansion of Rastafari whose following had representation—Nyabinghi, Bobo Ashanti, Twelve Tribes, and Non-Affiliated. Gideon wanted nothing to do with the initiative because it wasn't his to lead. So the church forfeited their opportunity to be included in the reorganizing exercise.

The center of Temple Yard was established as a communal meeting point. It housed a small amphitheater for concerts, lectures, movie nights, and community discussions. During the restructuring period, mostly everything in Temple Yard was determined, designed, and built by the people of Temple Yard.

Eventually, Shotta Forward not only opened Vital Too, but brought vitality back to Temple Yard, now beautified with plants, artwork, and charming shop spaces. The Yard was alive like never before, pulsing with music, whether drumming, live performances, or a sound system DJ. Irie to all, people poured into Temple Yard on a daily basis to purchase goods or just to gather in the Rasta oasis in the heart of Bridgetown.

Vital Too was located in the quarter that housed the Non-Affiliates. The line leading to Vital Too's bright red food truck never seemed to shorten. Marley was sitting at a table off to the side, waiting for I-Am to join her, when Duti video called from Trinidad.

"Hey, stranger," she answered.

"Hey, Marley. Ah, look at you, showing off on me. Where you are looks nice," he greeted her.

"No one is showing off on you," Marley replied.

"Yuh cheating on me with some new art?" Duti queried playfully.

"No. I'm here in Temple Yard, eating lunch and waiting for I-Am," Marley responded with a giggle. "That gorgeous mural in the background is just part of the vibe of the place. It's how we do down here in the Yard. When you get back, I'll bring you across for the experience and to meet the artists who created it. They are some real Irie ones."

"That sounds good. Respect."

"How are things with you? Were you able to work stuff out?" Marley followed up.

"Yeah. Everything is pretty much organized on this end. I honestly didn't expect that I would have been away so long, if at all. I'll be back tomorrow afternoon. Can you pick me up from the airport?"

"Sorry. I can't. I'm at the station until two p.m. I'll ask Zenobia to collect you, though."

"Sweet. I just sent you my flight details."

"I'll forward them to her now before I forget."

"Thanks. Really appreciate it. This was a quick link, though. Gotta run," Duti said, wrapping up the conversation.

"No worries," Marley assured.

"Peace."

"One love."

Marley finished off her curry veg wrap. She was observing the bustle of the market when I-Am finally joined her.

"Love and light, sis," I-Am offered Marley when she finally reached their meeting spot. Marley looked drained but immediately became refreshed in her sistren's presence.

"Love and light to you, as well," Marley genuinely offered in return. "How are you and the baby doing? You all good?" Marley queried, realizing how stressful these events must have been on I-Am.

"We good. He's in there chilling," I-Am reported as she stroked her belly with her right hand while pressing down on her nostril with her left thumb as she drew a breath through her Vicks inhaler. "Earlier, he was kicking up a storm. But he like he tired out heself. No worries yuh sight. Everything bless."

They hugged and then sat quietly, happy to be in each other's company, opting not to discuss any of what transpired the day in front. Marley had put on a happy face for Duti, but she wasn't anywhere near happy. All day long, she kept reliving excerpts from Sunday's episode. Nubya, trembling and terrified. Judah, badly wounded and unconscious. At least those parts she could make sense of. But Lee Mile, she had no words for that experience.

Marley was tired at most, angry at least. Added to that, all of the mix-up business with the coconut tree. What was that about? Nubya was a bona fide. They were even in business together. Trying to work it out, Marley reasoned that neither of those two factors meant that Nubya had to reveal the inner workings of her life to her. Nowadays, people tended to overshare, seldom reserving anything for themselves.

Marley couldn't fault Nubya for having a private life with Judah. That was her husband. Just saying the statement out loud in her head, Marley heights the ludicrousness of her thinking.

The music on the radio that was playing from the speaker next to the food truck halted. A reporter interrupted the song to announce a breaking news story.

"This now in," the important-sounding voice notified the listeners. "The body of an unidentified man was discovered this morning. Official police reports state that the male, who appears to be in his early thirties, was found lying naked on the side of a cart road on Bath Hill, St. John, just after ten o'clock. The body of the deceased appeared to have sustained a bullet wound to the chest. Police are asking anyone with information to come forward and assist with the investigation."

"You hear that?" I-Am whispered to Marley, outwardly nonchalant, but channeling the intensity of her enthusiasm across the table through her eyes. Marley put on her game face and responded, as if hearing the horrible news for the first time.

"It's tonight they're going?" Marley asked I-Am in a semi-hushed tone.

"Yeah, that's what we agreed," I-Am confirmed.

"Remind them to be careful. One prediction down. One more to go."

DO FUH DO AIN'T OBEAH

Konjah Man and Shotta Forward returned to Judah's house on Tuesday. They wanted to get there before the evening was dark enough to trigger the security lights.

Leaving the house after Sunday's shooting, Konjah Man had latched the top lock of the side paling door. So he and Shotta Forward now had to go through the house to enter the backyard. Evening always came early in St. John. Relying on the residual daylight, Shotta Forward scanned the yard for the coconut tree Nubya had described. Eventually, he spotted it in the far corner of the yard. Tall, with a curved trunk that bent skyward, the massive central mango tree had shielded it from view.

The coconut tree's trunk was actually growing from outside of the paling, even though its top crowned with cascading leaves and bunches of coconuts dangled high above the yard. Konjah Man strapped a pair of cleats, which Judah kept in his shed, onto his shoes, before heading over to link up with Shotta Forward. To get out of the yard, he went through the trick door with the hidden exit that was built into the outdoor bamboo shower.

For all the years that Konjah Man had known Judah, all the times he had cleaned herb at his house—sat in the yard to burn, reason, or chill—he never once knew the extent of Judah's full setup. Hide things in plain sight, Judah always reasoned. But ganja stashed right over his head, camouflaged in bags tucked out of view between bunches of coconuts. Simply genius.

Konjah Man attached a rope to the burlap bags that hid the stash of Stinga's taxed ganja and lowered them to Shotta Forward. He climbed back down the tree trunk, sealed the bamboo door, and returned the cleats to the shed. Outside was still bright enough to see when they locked the front door to make their getaway. But stepping off of the veranda, the security lights flicked on, causing the men to tense a bit.

Shotta's senses were heightened from the enchantment the mystic woman at Lee Mile's house had covered him with after sending him the intention to follow her through the archway. Passing through to the other side, Shotta Forward found himself surrounded by endless dunes of glistening sand that shimmered in the radiance of the location's ambient light.

It was just the two of them. Shotta and the mystic woman, in the middle of this strange stretch of desert, punctuated by clusters of dunes. The sound of the ocean gave the impression that it was nearby, but it was nowhere to be seen. Shotta Forward followed the mystic woman, who was now trekking up the ridge of a dune. Everything around him appeared golden and alive. From the blond stretch of the open expanse above him, all the way until it bowed down to touch the undulating horizon in the distance.

The mysterious woman halted. Looking over her shoulder, she sent Shotta Forward another intention. The next thing he knew, he was kneeling in the sandy slope he moments ago was hiking on.

Shotta Forward's head was spinning. What was this woman doing to him? He didn't like it. Feeling for his gun, he dislodged it from his waist. It felt heavy, like lead in his hand. In this place of brilliance, he wasn't feeling well at all. The experience was all too confusing. Try as he could, Shotta Forward couldn't fight it.

His fingers fumbled. He managed, however, to cock his gun. In a daze, he found the silhouette of the woman he had followed across the sand. She was right in front of him. The curve of her waist leading into her hips at eye level to his gaze. She looked down at Shotta Forward, filling his view of the sky with the fullness of her upper body as she peered out from behind a pair of breasts that mimicked the curvature of the dunes that surrounded them.

"This will protect you," she conveyed to Shotta Forward, who looked up in full submission to the glistening enchanter, cupping his face in her hand. Crouching over him, she gently blew upon his face. In return, a golden glow ascended from his eyes. Shotta Forward's weapon slipped from his grip as he melted into the magnetism of her embrace.

The yard light had momentarily spooked them. Shotta Forward felt a familiar presence manifest and an awareness touched him. Post-hesitation, Shotta Forward and Konjah Man quickly proceeded to Judah's gate and quietly made their descent down the climb. Reaching the bottom steps, they surveyed their surroundings with a quick glance. Promptly, the two men headed over to Konjah Man's food van, which they had used in hopes of not raising further suspicions. The community was still thirsting for an explanation of Sunday's events. On top of that, Monday morning brought news of a naked dead body found in a nearby cart road. Things were getting out of hand.

Shotta Forward caught wind of the ambush first when a golden flash cut across his eyes. He turned his attention in the direction of three masked men, making ready to ambush him in an approach from the opposite side of the road. Shotta Forward barely had time to pull his weapon.

"Guns!" he shouted, reaching into his waist.

At once, the men started shooting. Shotta and Konjah simultaneously made a grand leap away from the direction of the gunmen. They managed to crawl to shelter behind the paling of Ms. Ashby's shop just a few feet away. A shower of bullets followed closely, reverberating off of the zinc fence paling, sounding like a crude rendition of some amateur playing an untuned steel pan. Shotta Forward popped out from behind the paling and managed to fire two shots at the assailants. The third bullet pierced the shoulder of one of his targets.

Konjah Man tugged at Shotta and signaled for him to follow in his direction. Ducking, they ran along the ridges of the paling, in the opposite direction of the open fire, with Shotta Forward licking off bullets in the direction of the pursuers to keep them off their trail.

At the end of the paling, they both turned left to circle around, heading toward the main road, which placed them on the opposite side from the shooters. Approaching the scene, a van rushing down the road pulled up shortly ahead of them. Three men from the Revolutionary Action Syndicate bailed out onto the street, shooting in a reverse ambush of the men who had first opened fire.

Seeing this, Konjah Man approached the road. Placing his index fingers on his lips, he belted out their signature call. The man nearest heard and turned running in Konjah Man's direction. The van immediately followed.

"There are three of them," Shotta Forward revealed as his soldier, who had rushed past Konjah Man to reach him, briskly stooped down by his side.

"Come this way!" Shotta Forward commanded his soldier, as he threw the burlap bags that he had in his possession in Konjah Man's direction.

Konjah Man grabbed the bags and ran across the street, jumping into the getaway van just as it started to accelerate down the road.

Shotta Forward and his soldier tacked back to re-enter the gunfight. The two gunmen who were in pursuit, rounded the corner and ran right into Shotta Forward and his soldier's guns, pointed, aiming straight at them. Wanting to live, the assailants dropped their weapons on sight just as two bullets each entered their upper bodies and legs. Shotta Forward always left his victims with the marks of his signature style of injury. For him, there was no need to kill.

Shotta's soldiers gathered the two wounded hooligans and dragged them back to the other side of the paling, where the third injured gunman had been disarmed and lay defeated, face-down on the ground. Konjah Man had tacked back, having delivered the burlap bags of herb to Zaire at a meeting point not far away. Witnessing the victory upon his approach, he sounded the signal again, waiting for a response before coming around Ms. Ashby's shop.

Miraculously, Konjah Man's van only caught two bullet holes. He and Shotta Forward quickly climbed in to make their escape. Shotta's soldiers leapt back into the vehicle they had arrived in.

Looking out of the window at the injured men lumped together pathetically on the ground, Shotta Forward cautioned, "Let this beef die, or you will," before peeling off down the road, leaving the injured bandits where they lay.

24

MUSIC. MESSAGE. FORWARD

"That's right. 'Protect me people, Jah, nuh mek dem get caught inna crossfire,'" Lady Khando chimed in as Tarrus Riley's song "Wildfire" began to wind down. The stress of the past few days was piling on. Judah being ambushed on Sunday. Now a hit on Konjah Man and Shotta Forward last night. She hadn't slept properly, either, with work demands and her personal life battling for attention during her waking hours.

"So much craziness is happening right now. Fellas, be cool. Things are getting out of hand," she continued.

The song's chorus butted back in. DJ Kutlass signaled to Khando that it was time for the next segment.

"It's fifteen minutes past the hour, and that means it's time for our Wednesday morning 'Talk Yuh Talk!' session. Callers, you know how this goes. The rules are: You have one minute to vent. No cussing or bad-mouthing anyone. Just straight up speak your mind. Speak your heart. Stick to the facts. In exchange, you get to say what you want to say, without interruption. Our number here is two-four-B-L-A-Z-E. Call in. Phone lines are open."

By the time Lady Khando had finished her piece, DJ Kutlass had a caller already lined up to go on air. "Lady Khando, we have a caller on the line. Good morning, welcome to BLAZE-HD 98.3FM. You are on the air. Talk Yuh Talk!"

The callers were really going in on their topics. Zoe was monitoring the comments on the live feed. Kutlass was engaged with the phone lines. Everyone sensed that Lady Khando was really having a rough week. So they tried to lift some of her load, leaving her just to govern the radio announcements.

"… Plant marijuana and secure the economy. Let's get real!" The caller was now in full petition mode. "Feed our citizens, work the land, lower the number of imports, and show the people of this nation a new direction. Our politicians act as if dem is some kind of foreign moles, looking out for someone else's agenda, and it shows. Barbados is going to suffer if we don't get our heads right. The world is legalizing marijuana use; meanwhile, we down here, sitting around waiting for a failing tourism market to pick up. You realize what the attorney general telling you, though? He's saying that we can't legalize marijuana 'cause we don't know enough about it. We have to do the research before we can make a decision.

"So, wait! He 'bout hey locking up people's children, brothers, and child fathers for something he doesn't know the fullness of, and we 'bout hey taking it just so? Not a boy ain't find nothing strange 'bout that? Everybody just chilling?"

"Caller, thank you for your contribution," Lady Khando cut in just as the caller's time was up. "DJ Kutlass," she petitioned her sidekick.

"Yes, Lady Khando."

"That last caller was making some points, though," she instigated.

"It's true. I listened real close, and all I could do was count facts."

"Seriously, though, how is it that we are letting these government officials pull the wool over our eyes like this? Basically holding our livelihoods to ransom. You know that the majority of the 'so-called' gun violence would dissipate if we went the route of decriminalization?" Lady Khando reasoned.

"Lady Khando, in all fairness, I would have to agree with you. Look at places like Amsterdam and Vancouver, that have long ago decriminalized ganja use. They are not reporting any increases in crime; furthermore, their quality of life is tops. Their citizens are living in safe, crime-free environments, contrary to what is being said by our representatives."

"It's sad because we are down here on our island gem, living like dog eat dog, fighting over the most natural substance in the world—herb—simply because our policymakers, our politicians, lack the vision to carry us forward. To free the herb," Lady Khando rallied.

"Lady Khando, what *can* we do?" DJ Kutlass punched with his attempt at being funny.

"DJ Kutlass, we can learn from the ones who know that with decriminalization will come increased opportunity. If you're scared that crime is going to escalate just because a man can blowback a big one legally, fear not. Everyone knows that herb makes the people feel nice."

Just then, right on cue, DJ Kutlass dropped in the intro to Rita Marley's "One Draw."

"I want to get high, so high ... " Rita Marley's reggae hit lit up the airwaves.

Everyone in the studio laughed out loud, Marley included. She hadn't laughed from a good place since sitting in the kitchen Saturday past with her sistren, Nubya and I-Am.

She returned to the microphone. "It's twenty-eight minutes past the hour. We'll ride this Rita Marley classic down to our eight thirty news time. I'm Lady Khando, burning up the airwaves, and you are tuned into BLAZE-HD 98.3FM. Music. Message. Forward.

"DJ Kutlass, pull that one right up! Wheel and come again!"

25

YOU ARE BEAUTIFUL

"Hello, beautiful." Lee Mile brought his stallion to a trot as he lined up with the side of Marley's Jeep Wrangler Unlimited.

"Hi, handsome," Marley smiled up at him as she cruised along the road leading up to his property.

"Wow! I see that I'm back in your good graces," he responded, surprised. Holding onto the mane of the horse, he patted its side, encouraging it to keep pace with the vehicle.

"Who told you that you were out of them?" Marley teased back, allowing herself to soften in Lee Mile's presence.

"Alright. I'll leave that alone," he surrendered.

"I've always wanted to learn how to ride bareback, but it looks so hard," Marley admitted to Lee Mile.

"Yeah? You could learn. It's not as difficult as it looks," Lee Mile added.

"I don't know. It looks really challenging trying to contain such a powerful animal without the support of a saddle," Marley said.

"I can show you how if you want," Lee Mile offered smoothly.

"Hear you! We'll see," Marley said coyly.

"I'll meet you at the house?" he then prompted.

"Yeah, cool," Marley agreed.

Lee Mile cantered off toward his home. When Marley pulled into the driveway, he had already dismounted and had passed his stallion over to the groom. He waited patiently on the walkway to his house for Marley to park her Jeep and join him.

"I mean it," he said when she finally was standing by his side, "you *are* beautiful."

"Lee Mile," Marley blushed, a little puzzled by this return to his earlier declaration.

But he was serious. He hadn't made any movements to head into the house at all. Instead, right where he stood, in the hot sun, Lee Mile chose to have this conversation with Marley.

"If you can let a man have his life, you can be a part of that life," he said, looking across at her. Marley's face began to contort slightly as it weighed all that she wanted against all that she had been through, and all that she knew.

"What do you want?" he asked, probingly. "Because I know what I want."

"And what's that?" Marley challenged.

"This! Us! Just how we are, in our unique way. That works for me. Us. You and me," he reckoned.

Marley pondered his statement. She looked across to search his eyes and found sincerity. They had done this dance, on and off, for so long. Her reluctance to give in was the underlying problem.

It was one thing for her to be Marley, the radio personality, Lady Khando, gallery owner, and daughter of Mr. Cadogan. Those things, she was accustomed to. That person, she knew well. She was in control of that narrative. But out here in Lee Mile's world, she tended to feel like a fairy floating on clouds in a magical wonderland, which she had no way of controlling. Then there was the incident with him and Nubya. What was that?

On her long, silent drives between reality and Lee Mile's universe, she had resolved that there was no reference point for how to exist in his world. Out here, she was at the mercy of whim and fancy, and that scared her, muted her mind, and accelerated her heart. In this place, she was a different kind of beautiful. A different kind of Marley.

"I dare you," Lee Mile finally challenged.

"What?"

"I dare you," he repeated.

"Seriously?" she responded. Like always, she was out of her depth with him.

"Yes. I dare you to love me as I am, and us as we are." Lee Mile leaned in to her. He wanted her to see him. To know that it was okay. He was here. Even in his absence, he was never truly gone. No matter what he manifested, there was nothing for her to fear.

"You scared me."

"I would never hurt you."

"I can't do this ..."

"Or you won't."

Slightly sweaty, Lee Mile's skin sparkled under the blazing sunlight. He reached out and lovingly drew Marley nearer to him. He wanted her to feel him. He wanted to be closer to her. She wanted things to make sense, so she could file them away neatly in her understanding of life.

Tenderly, Lee Mile held Marley under the brutal heat of the midday sun. It was hard not to inhale him. Caught in his orbit, to her, he smelled like freshly tilled earth. In full adoration of the flower in his arms, Lee Mile planted a kiss on Marley's quivering lips, as if she were all he had ever needed in this world.

26

PORT SAINT LUCIE

Down by the docks of the marina, Nubya and Marley held each other in a long embrace, onboard the flybridge of Mr. Cadogan's MCY-80. Judah lounged on an ample plush leather sofa across from where the two women were standing, exchanging their goodbyes. In the luxury of his surroundings onboard the yacht, he sat in quiet reflection.

Judah absorbed the view of the posh residences that lined the marina from the privacy of his vantage point in the flybridge's solarium. He was happy to be alive. Looking at Judah spread across the sofa, absorbing the salty fresh breeze whenever it dipped down through the sunroof to play in the shade cast by the tinted windows around him, you couldn't tell. The neutral set of his chiseled features guarded the complexity of what it really meant to be Judah on the inside. His wounds had healed substantially, but he was still weak. Since the attack, his body felt foreign to him. Almost new, as if he were occupying it for the first time.

In Lee Mile's care, Judah felt healed in a place deep

down inside where he was never brave enough to go. During his short stay at the ranch, Lee Mile informally coached Judah in the art of shifting his shape, by adding dimension to the lessons Judah's father had never finished teaching him.

Judah now had the maturity to ably grasp the fullness of what was being taught under Lee Mile's supervision. He was a long way from the teenager trying to make sense of his father's abstract references that he made on the lengthy, adventurous walks they often took through the forest.

Many of his father's teachings were wrapped in parable-like stories, told to a young Judah while seated in front of fiery sunsets. Judah still remembered the crunchy feeling between his toes of the coarse black volcanic sand, from the beachfront of his childhood home on the outskirts of Kingstown, St. Vincent. The timbre of voices of the fishermen surrounding him, knowledgeable in the ancient ways, cloaking their command of the sciences under the mundane simplicity of their everyday lives. These random memories lingered fresh in Judah's mind. Residue from a lifetime long ago.

Lee Mile advised Judah to relax extensively until he was truly strong. Not only in will, but in body and spirit as well. Judah's physical recovery was remarkable but shouldn't be taken for granted.

On the morning they departed his house for the marina, Lee Mile gave Judah a leather pouch with a mix of dried bushes in it. From a pinch of the contents, he prescribed that Judah brew a tea, of which he was to sip a portion daily, during the darkest hour of the night. Lee Mile warned Judah that when the pouch was finally empty, it would be time for Judah to pay him another visit.

"This will help you also," Lee Mile further explained. He handed Judah a thin, twenty-four-karat-gold rope chain, with an unusual ring hanging from it.

"What's this for?" Judah asked, puzzled by the gift.

"That's for your skin. Gold has a way of monitoring your health. It's a natural indicator of if something isn't right with your body. If the chain starts to turn black, something is off. Remove the ring and place it on whichever finger it fits. The ring knows where to go and what to do. Once your chain returns to its natural color, put the ring back on it. Never take this chain to be cleaned by a jeweler. Don't try to clean it yourself, either."

Looking at Lee Mile absorbingly, Judah was processing what he was being told.

"This is not that type of jewelry," Lee Mile concluded.

"Sight." Judah nodded in acknowledgment. He flashed Lee Mile a rare sighting of a smile that brought his eyes to life with a boyish innocence in the unguarded moment.

"Put it on now," Lee Mile suggested.

Judah fastened the chain around his neck, then tucked it under the t-shirt he was wearing beneath his tracksuit.

"Give thanks I-yah. Real talk." Judah saluted Lee Mile, placing his hand over his heart in sincere appreciation. "De father definitely does work through you in mysterious ways."

"Daddy is heading over to Carriacou first to pick up my mother." Marley's voice filtered into Judah's thoughts, bringing him back to the present. "It seems they've decided to make an event out of this trip since they are taking you guys to St. Vincent. Hope you don't mind making a few stops in the Grenadines along the way." Marley opened up her conversation with Nubya to include Judah and his silence.

"Marley, you are too much." Nubya smiled back at her friend sincerely. "We are grateful. Thanks so much for looking out for us."

It was agreed that Judah and Nubya needed to let things cool down a little on the homefront. It was Judah's idea to head over to St. Vincent for the timeout. Stinga might hold sway in Barbados, but Judah was respected in St. Vincent. Marley, thinking that flying would be too stressful, asked her father if they could use his yacht. Turns out he was already heading in that direction for a rendezvous with Mrs. Cadogan. Being the father that he was, he had no problem taking her friends along for the ride.

"Marley ..." Judah slowly eased off of the couch and approached her. "Sis, I owe you my life," he admitted shyly.

It was rare for Marley to be lost for words. But in this moment, she was. "Everything bless," she replied to the man she thought she knew but came to learn she had no clue about. "Can I hug you?" The old Marley surfaced.

Judah never allowed for close personal contact of any kind. He deemed such casual contact inappropriate between members of the opposite sex. But on this day, in Judah's eyes, Marley was no longer a sistren, but his sister. The brief embrace made everyone laugh.

"I-Am and I will handle things on this end. So no worries. You guys relax, heal, and come back when you feel ready to," Marley reassured.

She made her way to the stairs to descend to the main deck. Marley took one last look at her friends before making her descent. Nubya started to cry. Marley couldn't restrain her tears, either, and they came out to meet Nubya's.

"We good," Marley insisted, gently taking her friend into her arms one last time.

"I know," Nubya sniffled, recharging in the tender embrace of her sistren.

"Thanks a million for everything." Nubya smiled into Marley. "I love you so much." Nubya's words fluttered across to Marley's heart.

"I know. I love you, too, Bella Bella."

27

RASTAMAN WHEEL OUT

Marley was sitting backstage with DJ Kutlass going through notes for the show, when I-Am entered their tent.

"Can we come in?" I-Am asked, poking half of her protruding body through the tent's side opening.

"Yes, you and your tummy may enter," Marley replied with a broad smile plastered across her face.

"Love and light, sis. You look absolutely stunning!" I-Am declared as they embraced.

"Thank you. It's a Nubya original, of course," Marley announced proudly.

"As is my outfit," DJ Kutlass interjected. Everyone chuckled because he was wearing a plain white V-neck t-shirt, matched with a pair of white jeans, all of which he had bought online.

"Kutlass, you are too much!" I-Am responded, punctuating her statement with a steups.

Just then, a production assistant stuck her head into the

tent to make an announcement. "DJ Kutlass and Lady Khando, we are ready for you. You're on in five minutes."

"Cool," DJ Kutlass responded to the assistant. He shot Marley a probing look.

"We good," Marley said, dismissing DJ Kutlass's concerns.

"Yeah, man," he replied. "But are *you* good?" he asked, walking over and placing his hands on her arms as he looked into her face to see for himself if she was really alright.

"Yes. I'm safe. No need to worry," Marley assured.

"Cool." Giving her a quick brotherly hug, DJ Kutlass made his way out of the tent.

"Meet you by the stairs in two minutes," Marley called out to him as he disappeared into the loudness of the night.

"Marley," I-Am began to query, but Marley cut her off.

"I-Am. I'm good. Okay?"

"Okay."

"How do I look?" Marley asked, turning slowly for I-Am to see the fullness of her outfit.

"You look I-tiful!" I-Am beamed, taking two draws from her Vicks inhaler. Marley took a quick look in the mirror. Happy with what she saw, she and I-Am made their way out of the tent and into the bustle of backstage activities to meet up with Kutlass.

Wending her way through the crowd, Marley fielded a bunch of greetings from different colleagues before joining DJ Kutlass, who was waiting at the bottom of the stairs by the side of the stage. The night was charged with excitement, emanating from everyone. Marley could feel jolts of anticipation and anxiety streaming through her body, keeping her on edge.

"Sis …" The voice caught Marley's attention just as the production assistant placed a microphone in her hand.

"Shotta!" Marley smiled, reaching out to hug him as he approached.

"Everything bless?" he asked.

"Everything blessed," she replied.

"You have to go on now," the production assistant interrupted.

Marley turned and smiled endearingly at Shotta Forward, then nodded to DJ Kutlass that she was ready to start the show.

Taking the lead up the stairs, Marley began to feel her heart thumping loudly behind the enclosure of her ribs. The whirlwind of events from the past few days momentarily caught up with her, snatching her breath for a second.

Behind her, DJ Kutlass caught the feeling that Marley was about to miss her cue. So he took the lead and shouted into the microphone. "*Barbados!*"

They reached the top of the stairs just as the amped crowd screamed back in acknowledgment. Crossing the stage, Marley regained her composure as she arrived at her mark. "How are you feeling?" she queried.

The crowd went wild with excitement. She had never seen anything like it! The stage was huge, even with the setup of a full band. The stadium, impressive. From her vantage point, the crowd looked thick, seeming to stretch for miles across the arena. She felt on top of the world. Like she was riding the night's energy as it poured across the venue, lifting her spirit.

"I'm Lady Khando," Marley introduced herself smartly.

"And I'm DJ Kutlass."

"We're told that there are twenty-seven thousand reggae lovers here tonight at the *Two Sevens Clash* show! Let me hear you make some noise!" Marley shouted.

The roar from the crowd was deafening. Looking past the laser-bright spotlights onto the grounds, then into the stands, Marley was mesmerized. The vibration from the crowd was intense. The love, overwhelming.

"It's Heroes Day, people! We know that you are here to see reggae royalty, Sizzla. Culture. Chronixx. Is that true?"

Another outburst of approval erupted from the crowd. On the big screen on either side of the stage, Marley caught a glimpse of the drone footage of the event as it was streaming live.

"Do you see that?" Marley asked, bringing the crowd's attention to the video feed on the screen. "That's us! I want to shout out Shotta Forward and RAS Entertainment, the Revolutionary Action Syndicate, for putting on this epic event. As of Wednesday, this show was officially sold out! Do you believe that? Pure niceness!"

"Real talk, Lady Khando. Nuff respect to a man like Shotta Forward and his team. You guys are always all about excellence," DJ Kutlass acknowledged. "Right about now, I know that you all are more than ready to party." DJ Kutlass began to hype the crowd. "Massive, are you ready? Say, 'Yeah!'"

"Yeah!" the crowd responded.

"Say, 'Yeah!'" Kutlass urged them again, turning his attention to the other end of the stage with his request.

"*Yeah*!" the audience shouted back.

"Well, officially, let me welcome you," Marley announced, taking on a reverent tone. Looking out onto the massive gathering, she tilted her head up and raised her voice as she extended a heartical welcome to the audience before her. "Greetings in the name of His Imperial Majesty, Haile Selassie I. Jah!"

The massive crowd in unison replied, "*Rastafari!*"

GLOSSARY

Babylon: a corrupt system of government or society's status quo; Rastafari word for the police; may also be used to describe any person or organization that oppresses the innocent

Bailed out: to jump out of a moving vehicle

Bajan: a citizen of Barbados; slang for Barbadian

Bajan Green: Barbados cultivated marijuana, ganja, herb, or weed

Baje: short for Bajan or things related to it; an informal way of saying Barbadian, a Barbadian being a person from the Caribbean island of Barbados

Bales: marijuana packaged in sizable bundles for import/export activity

BDF: Barbados Defense Force; military

Block: a hangout spot for neighborhood men, usually located under a tree, backyard, by a shop, or near a corner store

Breddah: brother; could mean direct relation or a close friend

Bredren: brethren; slang for anyone who is a friend

Bud: unprocessed flower of the marijuana plant

Buck-pot: a cast iron pot traditionally used for cooking

Burn: the smoking of ganja

Cart road: informal road; dirt road

Catspraddle: to fall harshly; to land in an uncomfortable manner

Cha!: an exclamation expressing vexation, impatience, disappointment

Churchical: to be religious-like

Collins: alternative name for a cutlass or machete

Crown: Rasta locs; see locs

Daughter: term of endearment for a woman

De: the

Defense Force: Barbados Defence Force (BDF); Barbados' military

Dem: them or they

Dub: reggae/dancehall party

Fanta: (also called fronto, grabba, or hot grabba); a tobacco leaf

'Fore day: before the day

Fulljoy: happiness

Fyah: fire; sometimes used as a rebuke for evil

Gap: informal road; cart road

Gine: going to

Gree: agreed

Hail: a popular greeting exchanged by Rastas. Similar to saying, "Hello"

Hard-mouthed: miserly

Hawker: a peddler or vendor that mostly sells inexpensive goods, handicrafts, or food items on the streets or in a public market

Heartical: from the heart.

Heights: become aware of

Heights & Terraces: well-to-do neighborhoods

Hobby Class: freeloaders; free of cost; complimentary

I and I: Rasta speak; referring to the speaker and the presence of God

I-ration: nature

I-tiful: beautiful

I-yah: you

Ital: vegetarian-based Rastafari food that is in its natural state; does not contain any artificial elements; cooked with no salt

Ites: the color red

Jipsy: nosy; inquisitive

Johnny Law: police

Knox: Rasta method of cooking

Land: slang for the smuggling of illegal substances across borders; also see "Shot"; when someone turns up at a destination

Lick up: mash up; destroy

Licking off: the act of firing a gun, e.g., licking off a shot; to shoot

Liming: to hang out, chill, or relax somewhere with companions

Liveth: to be alive

Livity: lifestyle

Locs: a hairstyle defined by uncombed clumping of hair primarily associated with Rastafari but also worn by non-Rastas; commonly referred to as dreadlocks

Naggathon: excessive nagging or harassment

Nuff: a lot of

Obeah: Caribbean-type of sorcery of West African origin similar to Voodoo; a high science

Obeah Man: a high priest of Afro-Caribbean spiritual science who some view as witchcraft

Ones: associates

Order: rules

Overs: to fully comprehend; understand

Paling: a fence, oftentimes constructed from sheets of galvanized zinc

Pot-starver: a skinny dog with protruding ribs

Rab: unused

Rakey: oftentimes "poor rakey"; to look extremely lean due to malnutrition or neglect

Ramp: to associate or be involved with

Rasshole: an indigenous Barbadian/Bajan curse word

Reason: to have a conversation

Reasoning: the act of coming to an understanding through dialogue

Run: smuggling activity

Safe: okay; cool

Sap: soup

Screw: angry

Shot: slang for smuggling activity; also a gunshot

Sight: acknowledgement; understanding; to see or to get the point

Spliff: ganja rolled in smoking papers for smoking

Stash: to put away in secrecy

Steupse/stupse: also referred to as the kissing of or sucking of one's teeth; a sound that can be made jokingly to dismiss the importance of a statement being made; in serious situations, considered disrespectful and used to convey disregard for another person

SVG: the Caribbean islands of St. Vincent and the Grenadines

Tam: a round, crocheted cap worn by Rastas to tuck their locs away out of sight

Task Force: police special unit; local SWAT force

Tear down: to move or drive speedily

The Shark: Regional Security Services (RSS) airplane used for searching out drug activity in the Caribbean

Town: informal name for Bridgetown, the capital of Barbados

Vincy: slang for a person from the Eastern Caribbean islands of St. Vincent and the Grenadines

Weight: the possession of illegal substances in large amounts

Wolf down: eat quickly

Yard: an enclosed area of land, usually residential property, e.g., garden, courtyard, yard, etc.

Yeah man: yes

Yout': youth; young people; children